# TWO BROTHERS

BERNARDO ATXAGA, a Basque, was born in 1951. He published his first work at the age of twenty in an anthology of Basque writers. He has written plays, children's books, radio scripts and novels, including *Obabakoak*, which has been published in fourteen languages including English, and won several prizes. His most recent novel published in English by Harvill, *The Lone Woman*, was praised in the *New Statesman* by James Hopkin for its "taut, elegant sentences which generate a sense of restlessness and foreboding".

MARGARET JULL COSTA has translated three other novels by Bernardo Atxaga – *Obabakoak*, *The Lone Man* and *The Lone Woman*. Spanish writers whose work she has translated include Javier Marías (whose *A Heart So White* won the Dublin International IMPAC Award), Carmen Martín Gaite and Arturo Pérez-Reverte. Her translation of Fernando Pessoa's *The Book of Disquiet* won her the Portuguese Translation Prize and, in 2000, she was awarded the Weidenfeld Prize for her translation of José Saramago's *All the Names*.

*Bernardo Atxaga*

# TWO BROTHERS

## The Fourth Song

*Translated from the Spanish by*
*Margaret Jull Costa*

THE HARVILL PRESS
LONDON

First published in Spanish with the title
*Dos Hermanos* by Ollero & Ramos,
Madrid, 1995

First published in Great Britain in 2001 by
The Harvill Press,
2 Aztec Row, Berners Road
London N1 0PW

www.harvill.com

1 3 5 7 9 8 6 4 2

This edition has been translated with the financial assistance
of the Spanish Dirección General del Libro y Bibliotecas,
Ministerio de Cultura

Bernardo Atxaga asserts the moral right to be
identified as the author of this work

A CIP catalogue record for this book
is available from the British Library

ISBN 1 86046 834 9

Typeset in Poliphilus at
Libanus Press, Marlborough, Wiltshire

Printed and bound in Great Britain by Butler & Tanner
at Selwood Printing, Burgess Hill

A man or a stone or a tree will begin
the fourth song.

*Les Chants de Maldoror*, Lautréamont

# CONTENTS

# THE BIRD'S STORY

*Concerning the inner voice. A death and a promise.*
*Paulo and Daniel*

THERE IS A VOICE that comes from deep within ourselves, and just as summer was beginning, when I was still an inexperienced bird and had never strayed far from the tree where I lived, that voice gave me an order. Before I heard the voice, I knew very little of the world: I knew the tree and the rushing stream beneath it, but almost nothing else. The other birds in my flock used to talk of houses and roads and about a huge river into which the waters of our stream and those of many others all flow, but I had never been to those places and did not know them. Nevertheless, I believed what they told me because the different descriptions tallied – the roofs were always red and the walls were always white and the huge river was always called the sea.

There is a voice that comes from deep within ourselves, the other birds told me. A voice unlike any other, a voice that has power over us.

"How much power?" I asked one day.

"We have to obey the voice," replied the birds who were at that moment resting amongst the branches of the tree.

3

But they couldn't be more specific, for not even the older birds had ever actually heard that powerful voice. They knew of its existence not from personal experience, but from what they had been told by other birds from other times. They believed in it, though, as surely as they believed in the existence of houses, roads and the sea. For my part, I took it to be just another story and didn't give it much importance, never dreaming that the voice would speak to me. Then, on that day at the beginning of summer, everything changed.

I felt suddenly very restless, the way birds do who are hungry or ill, and I spent the whole morning hopping aimlessly about the tree. This restlessness was combined with the unpleasant feeling that my ears had gone completely mad and were hearing things in a strange, disorderly fashion: the waters of the stream seemed to thunder over the pebbles; the birds nearby sounded to me as if they were screaming; the wind, which was no more than a breeze, was as deafening as a storm. Around midday, I began to experience difficulties breathing and I was suddenly alone. The other birds left the tree and flew off somewhere else.

"Why are you flying away from me?" I asked one of the last to go.

"Because you're dying," came the reply.

Convinced of the truth of that response, I decided to review my life. But my life until then had been so brief that the review only lasted a moment. Then I looked up at the sky, and its blue colour seemed to me more remote than ever. So I looked down at the stream, and the sheer speed of the water frightened me. Finally, I looked at the ground, at the brambles and nettles covering it, and into my head came a story I once heard about a girl who had fallen ill. Apparently, the doctor went over to the bed where she was lying and said:

"A torn skirt can be mended, but not this young girl's health. There's nothing to be done."

Her relatives did not tell her the truth, but decided to take her to a folk healer. After examining her, he said:

"There's nothing I can do. Her legs are swollen and her breathing is weak. She'll be dead within a couple of months."

They said nothing to the girl then either, because they did not want to cause her needless suffering. They put her on a horse and carried her back home. But time passed, and she eventually realised there was no hope for her. One evening, her brother found her in the garden crying.

"What's wrong, sister?" he said. And she replied:

"Nothing's wrong. I was just thinking that I'm still only nineteen and that soon I'll be buried under the earth."

That was the story I was remembering as I waited for the push that would propel me off the branch and onto the ground. Except that death did not come. Instead, I heard the voice. First, I felt the strident noises gradually dwindling away to nothing, and then a great silence filled the tree and its surroundings, like the silence that comes when snow covers the fields.

"Follow the road to Obaba and fly to Paulo's house," I heard someone say. It was a voice that seemed to emerge from the centre of that silence and from the centre of myself, from both places at once.

"I don't know where Obaba is and I don't know who Paulo is either," I thought, and just then I saw a village of about a hundred houses, Obaba, and near that village a sawmill and above that, on a small hill, a house with many windows. I knew at once – because the voice gave me that ability, that of seeing and knowing things by sheer power of thought – that this was Paulo's house.

I set off to carry out the order the voice had given me and I flew down the valley until the stream became as broad and deep as a river, and then I flew on above the alder trees, which, in places like Obaba, always accompany the river down to the sea. After a while, I noticed that the river was forming into a pool, and that the line of alder trees gave way to make room for a building surrounded by wooden logs and by piles of planks, and I knew that this was the sawmill and that my first journey was about to end. It was evening, and the sky was yellow and blue, intense yellow where the sun was setting and pale blue everywhere else.

I flew higher up, looked down and saw the two parts of Obaba, its four or five streets, its square, and then, again, the sawmill, the hill and the house of many windows. The roof of the house was red and its walls white. But what struck me more than the colours was the racket made by all the dogs in the area. They kept howling and barking.

"What are they making so much fuss about?" I thought.

I knew then that the cause of all the racket was the dog who was guarding the house of many windows, Paulo's house, for it was that dog's frantic howling and barking that was provok-ing the response from the other dogs. For some reason, perhaps because the voice inside me told me so, I associated the dogs' unease with what the sick girl had said to her brother:

"Nothing's wrong. I was just thinking that I'm only nineteen and that soon I'll be buried under the earth."

I did not need any more memories. I understood that the barking and howling announced a death.

"Paulo's death?" I wondered. I could not ignore the fact that the cause of all the commotion was there, at the door of his house. It was his dog that was howling and barking.

Where the sun had just set, the sky was growing red. The day was ending. And the life of someone who was living in the house of many windows was also ending. While I was thinking about this, I followed the course of the river with my eyes and I saw how it wound about the mountains until, at last, after crossing fields planted with corn, it surrendered its waters to the sea. In the sea – I could see them clearly – black fish were swimming.

Nevertheless, despite the ability which allowed me to perceive as images things that were far away or things that I was thinking or that the voice suggested to me, I could not penetrate the walls of Paulo's house to find out which member of the family was ill.

"Perhaps Paulo is the one who is dying. Perhaps that is why I'm here," I thought somewhat apprehensively.

I was still struggling with this idea when I heard a bell ringing. On the road linking the upper part of Obaba with the more heavily populated lower part that extended along both sides of the river, a boy dressed in red and white was ringing a bell, and all the men still working in the orchards and the fields knelt down as he passed. Behind the boy came a man dressed in black and bearing a cross, and behind him came a fairly large group of children.

"It's one of the signs of death," I thought, looking at the

7

procession. It seemed to be making its way towards the sawmill, towards the workers who, still in their overalls, stood together waiting, talking in low voices. Soon the bell in the tower started to ring and, as the gloomy sound rang out across the valley, the howling of the dogs grew more widespread and ever more frantic. I decided to fly down towards Paulo's house.

As soon as I approached, I saw a group of squirrels scurrying back and forth across the roof of the house and I immediately suspected the truth: that these squirrels had received the same order from the voice as I had. At first, it bothered me: Wasn't my presence enough? Did Paulo need more company?

The reply came at once. I learned that Paulo had an older brother, Daniel, and he was the reason the squirrels had come.

The first thing I noticed when I went into the house was the smell of wax polish on the gleaming wooden floors. Then I crossed a corridor and went into a room where a man was lying on the bed; his breathing was laboured. I realised that this was Paulo's father and that the boy beside the bed was Paulo himself.

"I beg you, please, Paulo, take care of Daniel. Never ever abandon him."

The man's eyes were closed, and he was tossing and turning in the bed. The sheets must have been burning hot.

"Why is it raining so heavily?" the man asked suddenly. "It's July, isn't it?"

It was July, and the sky I had just left behind me was certainly not a rainy sky. On the contrary, it had been a sunny day, and the light filtering in through the slats of the blinds was still bright enough to make the mirror on the wardrobe door glitter.

An old woman whom I hadn't noticed until then left the

8

corner where she was sitting and came over to the bed. I realised she was the woman who did the household chores.

"It's the dogs," she whispered. "The dogs are making him confused."

At that moment, the dog guarding the house was barking wildly, and his peers were answering him from every hallway in Obaba. In his delirium, Paulo's father was confusing the barking with the sound the rain made when it beat on the skylight in the roof.

"Take care of Daniel," the father said again, still without opening his eyes. "Take care of your brother at all times, come rain or shine, in July and all year round. You're only sixteen, and I hate to place such a heavy burden on your shoulders, but I have no choice, Paulo. I will be dead soon, and you will be the only one who can take it on. Someone else can look after the house, someone else can look after the sawmill, but, without you, Daniel will have no one. It's not your fault, Sara, as I've told you many times, and, besides, Daniel isn't a bad person."

It seemed that at any moment he might run out of breath.

"Sara isn't here," said the old lady, slightly raising her voice. "You're not talking to your wife, you're talking to your son."

"I'll soon be with Sara again," said the man. Paulo was staring at the mirror; he was very pale.

There was a silence, and the smell of sweat coming from the sick man's bed grew more intense, masking the smell of wax polish on the wooden floor. Paulo moved the leg he had been sitting on and rubbed it to get rid of the pins and needles.

"It wasn't your fault, Sara," said the man again.

"Talk to Paulo," said the old woman sternly, forcing the

man to open his eyes. Paulo swallowed hard and looked into those eyes. As his father's illness progressed, they had grown enormous, almost round.

"Daniel is your responsibility," said the man in an almost inaudible voice. "Don't just throw him away as if he were an old rag. He may not be normal, but he's not an old rag either. He's your brother, the only one you have."

The man sat up in bed, raised his fists to his head and let out a moan.

"Do you promise, Paulo?"

Paulo was incapable of saying a word, but he nodded firmly.

"He says he will," said the old lady. "Do you see? He's nodding. Don't worry, Paulo will take good care of his brother, and we'll help him."

Paulo left the room in which his father lay dying and searched the whole house for his brother Daniel. He found him at last in the kitchen, crouched under the table and staring at the wall with an expression that seemed to say: "This wall is the only thing I care about in all the world."

When Daniel heard the door opening, he crawled on his knees over to the wall and pressed his huge body against it. Although his intention had been to conceal himself more effectively, he merely succeeded in lifting the table up on his back so that it was resting on only three legs. Paulo accepted his brother's behaviour as if it were perfectly natural.

"What are you doing hiding under there, Daniel?" he said. There was a puddle of yellowish liquid on one of the floor tiles.

Daniel stopped staring at the wall and turned his head. He had almost no eyelashes and, in his wide eyes, there was an evident glint of fear. He was frightened by the dogs' endless howling and barking and because he had been left alone.

"Come on, Daniel, tell me, what are you doing?" Paulo said again.

The puddle was darkening on the tile, and the smell of urine was beginning to fill the air in the kitchen. Suddenly, Paulo spoke as if he too were a bird, that is, he translated his question into whistling, a long whistle for long words and a shorter one for short words, and this made his brother laugh. When Daniel laughed, he opened his mouth wide, revealing large, crooked teeth.

"Daniel is really ugly," I thought when I saw that mouth.

"Come on, Daniel! You should know by now that you're too big to hide from me, however hard you try."

Then he tickled him all over his great body and managed to get him out from beneath the table. Daniel was laughing like a madman and his guffaws echoed round the kitchen. Then, growing suddenly silent, he pointed to his trousers.

"I wet myself, Paulo."

He must have been no more than twenty, and his chest was already as big as the chests of two grown men. But, despite this, his voice was very weak, as if inside that great chest there was a pair of tiny lungs, capable of providing only enough air to pronounce those few words.

"What's our Daniel done then? Has he got a tap hidden in there somewhere?" asked Paulo with exaggerated gestures. Daniel was listening to him, giggling, squeezing between his thighs the tap Paulo had referred to.

"Right, out of those clothes this instant!" boomed Paulo,

11

pointing at his brother. Then he pinched him, and they both ran out into the corridor. Daniel was laughing raucously again, and his laughter seemed to bounce off the walls. No, his lungs were definitely not tiny.

"Gee up, horsey! Gee up!" shouted Paulo, climbing onto his brother's back, but his brother couldn't take his weight and, almost choking with laughter, he lay down on the floor and started clumsily wrestling. Where the two brothers tumbled and fought, the wax on the wood grew wet and dull. Finally, they both lay still. Sweat was pouring down Daniel's face, and he was breathing hard. Outside, the day had finally ended. The light filtered in through the balcony curtains and left pink stains on the floor and the walls.

Paulo's eyes remained fixed on one of those stains. They were the stains of summer. On days like this, his father used to wear a T-shirt to go to work at the sawmill. He had seen him go down there like that only twenty days ago. Now he was dying, and he would never see him again.

Paulo would have continued thinking his thoughts, but for the old woman who did the household chores. She closed the door of their father's bedroom, glided across the floor towards them and said:

"Shh, be quiet."

The old woman raised one finger to her lips. Paulo nodded and indicated one of the other doors along the corridor. She wasn't to worry, they weren't going to stay there. Then he helped his brother to his feet, and they both went into a nearby room, Paulo looking serious and Daniel laughing. When they got there, they found the squirrels.

They were sitting on the maroon bedspread nibbling a piece of bread. There were exactly six of them. When Paulo first saw them, he thought they were rats and was so frightened or so disgusted that he stepped back, treading on his brother's foot as he did so. Daniel didn't appear to mind and continued laughing. He was tall as well as fat, a whole head taller than Paulo.

The squirrels huddled together, looking like some strange animal with many eyes and many tails. Then they looked hard at the two heads framed in the doorway, to see which of the two was Daniel, the big one or the small one.

"Squirrels, Paulo!" screamed Daniel, going over to the bed. He was thrilled. "Are they for me, Paulo?" he asked, turning towards him.

"If they don't run away they are," replied Paulo, doubting that the animals would want to stay under their roof. He didn't know about the inner voice and would never have suspected that his brother was the reason the squirrels were there. They would definitely not be leaving.

"Can I play?" asked Daniel, picking up one of the squirrels in his hands, and, contrary to my expectations, doing so with great delicacy.

"Of course you can, Daniel, but first I have to change your clothes," said Paulo, going into a small adjoining room and returning with a bowl of water and a sponge.

Daniel lay down on the bed, and the six squirrels clustered round him. Paulo removed Daniel's shoes, trousers and under- wear, and then, after moistening the sponge, he began washing his brother's thighs. Daniel's thighs were pudgy and white as milk.

The barking of the dog guarding the house intensified and

became still more urgent. The dog seemed to be saying: "Let me off this chain and I'll destroy everything in my path." Immediately afterwards, someone knocked at the front door. Paulo hid the bowl and the sponge under the bed and pulled up his brother's trousers. Perhaps by imitation, the squirrels hid too.

The old woman who did the household chores walked past the bedroom, but came back to tell them to be quiet. Then she opened the front door, and a man dressed in black walked down the corridor as far as the room where the two brothers were. He was followed by the boy with the little bell.

"Here I am," said the man in black. "I've come to bring comfort to your father." He was, in fact, the same man I'd seen on the road. Despite his grey hair, he wasn't very old.

"Yes, sir," said Paulo, who felt embarrassed when the man tousled his hair. Paulo had fair hair.

"And what about our big boy, then? How's he doing?" the man asked, growing more cheerful and speaking more loudly. But Daniel was looking under the bed and did not even hear him.

"I must go and see your father, but I'll be right back," said the man in black as he left the room. The boy with the bell peered in and winked at Paulo. The squirrels clambered back onto the bed.

"They're going to give him the last rites, Daniel," said Paulo, lying down next to his brother and slipping his arm under his head. Daniel began playing with the squirrels, but more quietly this time.

"Shall I bring you some clean underwear?" said Paulo.

"Yes," said Daniel.

But they were very tired, and before Paulo could go and fetch the clothes, they both fell asleep.

14

# THE BIRD'S STORY CONTINUES

*The thoughts and preoccupations of a priest*

PAULO AND DANIEL WERE sleeping, and even I dozed off. After a while, when the house was at its most silent, a door closed, and there was the clatter of someone falling over in the corridor, followed by the loud tinkle of a bell.

"The boy who came with the man in black has slipped on the waxed floor and fallen over," I deduced.

The boy was obviously not badly hurt. He opened the front door and ran off down the hill, towards the sawmill, towards the village. The dog bade him farewell with a few barks that seemed to say: "If you don't watch out, I'll tear your throat out. Just don't let me see you around here again, especially not at night." But he soon grew tired of barking, and the house fell silent once more.

I had never known a more oppressive silence: the air thickened, the doors and windows seemed to be sealed tight shut, the space in the room grew smaller. Was that silence going to suffocate us? No, not us, but Paulo and Daniel's father. Indeed, it already had.

"They've fallen asleep," said the old woman, standing at

the bedroom door. "They've tired themselves out playing. You know what Daniel is like, he's always ready to play."

"Yes, he's a very playful boy," said the man in black, who appeared at the old woman's side. "Do they usually sleep together?" he asked.

"No, not usually," said the old woman, shaking her head. "They each have their own room."

"I see," said the man thoughtfully. "I'll stay here for a while. You start preparing the body."

The man went and sat by the bedroom window. He too was tired and in need of sleep. But instead he bowed his head and set to thinking about events in the present and in the past, going backwards and forwards, or forwards and backwards, not lingering long over anything on the way. He thought first about Paulo and Daniel's parents, regretting that they had both died before their one normal child had had time to grow up. Then his thoughts drifted off to the work being carried out in the cemetery, which was going to prove very expensive, and then shifted to the trees growing near the cemetery, cherry trees that always produced their fruit around the twenty-fourth of June, St John's day. At precisely that moment, I began to see the images inside the man in black's head.

First, I saw the tower in the upper part of Obaba, which he in his thoughts called the church, and, immediately afterwards, the inside of that tower. There, next to a wall full of statues, a man in glasses, with short-cropped hair, was playing the harmonium and occasionally conducting with one hand the singing of a group of ten boys. I noticed that one of the singers looked very much like the man in black and I deduced that it was in

fact him as a boy of only thirteen or fourteen. I deduced too —
from the words he used to think with — that both were priests.
The one playing the harmonium was a priest from the past; the
present-day priest was sitting by the bedroom window.

A local man came into the church. I saw him tell the boys
in the choir to stop singing, and then he went over to the priest.

"Sorry to interrupt you, Father," said the man. He spoke
very loudly, as deaf people tend to.

"Well, what brings you here?" replied the priest, stopping
his playing and holding out his hand to him. He seemed a very
good-humoured fellow.

"I wanted to ask you something," said the man, kissing the
priest's hand.

"Go on, then."

The boys in the choir were all very tense and were following
the conversation closely.

"Are these the boys who sang in the square on St John's eve?"

"They are," said the priest amiably. I had a fleeting image
of the square in Obaba with a great bonfire burning in the
middle. The ten boys in the choir were standing in that square
singing to the people who had come to enjoy the fiesta.

"Well, as you know, I own an orchard of cherry trees near
the cemetery. Now an odd thing happens to those cherry trees
year after year," said the man in a tone of voice that was
half-angry and half-amused. "When I look at it on St John's
eve, all the trees are laden with cherries. When I go there the
following morning, what do I see? Two or three of the trees
have been completely stripped of fruit. It's like magic. That's
why I've come to you, to see if you can offer some explanation."

19

"I see," said the priest, getting up from the harmonium and shooting an angry glance at the ten boys in the choir. "That mystery reminds me of another," he added.

"Oh, really," said the other man gravely.

"Well, after St John's eve, most of the boys you see here before you fail to turn up for rehearsal. I ask their parents what's wrong, and they tell me they're ill with stomach ache. What do you think? Does that seem odd to you?"

"Well, not really, because I know the effects of eating too many cherries. Especially if they're not quite ripe."

"Exactly," said the priest. Then he turned to the choir. "And what do you think?"

The boys lowered their eyes. After singing round the bonfire, and on the pretext of going up to the church to change their clothes, they always made a detour via the local man's cherry orchard. With everyone else in the square, they could pick fruit to their hearts' content.

"That's enough of that, lad, crying won't get you anywhere," said the priest, addressing the young priest-to-be. The other boys were all grave-faced, but they weren't crying. "It won't happen again," added the priest, looking at the man. "You can be quite sure of that. And if you ever need any help picking the cherries, you'll find a very good team right here."

"I'll bear that in mind," said the man.

"I know you're not really stealing," said the priest once the man had left. "You steal because one of you has the idea and because you've got energy to spare to get up to all kinds of mischief. But the harm you cause that man is real enough. He needs the fruit you throw away, because, of course, most of the cherries you don't even eat, you just throw them away. In fact, when I was out walking by the river the other day, I suddenly noticed that the millrace was full of little yellow balls. When I took a closer look, I saw that they were cherries."

After remembering these words, the thoughts of the priest by the window came to a halt, and I returned to the present, to what was happening in Paulo and Daniel's room. I saw that the priest was rubbing his eyes and face, as if to fend off sleep, and that he then looked out over the lights of Obaba. After a while, the bells in the church tower began gravely tolling.

"The bell is telling people that your father has died," he said, turning to the two brothers. Daniel stirred on the bed and breathed out loudly.

The priest studied him closely, as if searching for some sign or clue in that large, fat face, and then his thoughts began moving backwards again, towards the past, but very, very slowly now, as if the search for memories was painful to him. When he reached the point he was interested in, an image of the saw-mill came into my head or, rather, the image of a group of men loading planks onto a cart. The father of Paulo and Daniel was one of that group. Shortly afterwards, the carts were all loaded, and the father and the priest were talking in a room inside the mill.

"I've told you time and again," the priest was saying, "the Lord created your oldest son so that he would remain a child all his life; perhaps he should have tried a bit harder and made him a little angel instead. But I ask you as a friend and as a priest, please don't torment yourself over him."

21

"My wife used to say it was a punishment, and I think she was right. It was a terrible blow to us, we didn't deserve a monster like Daniel. At least Paulo came along straight afterwards. Paulo's a good boy."

"How can you talk about Daniel like that? How can you say he's a monster? You must put aside such ideas. You must convince yourself that he is just a large child, an innocent being who will always have the mind of a three-year-old."

"He's a three-year-old in some respects, but not in others," said Paulo and Daniel's father laconically.

"Don't believe everything people say," the priest retorted. Then he allowed himself to follow the idea that had just come into his head: he thought about the reputation Daniel had amongst some of Obaba's inhabitants, he thought about the mother who had come asking him to keep the boy away from her daughter and he thought lastly – and with some unease – about what was described as the boy's sexual appetite.

However, the boys' father was not referring to that, at least not exactly.

"He's started masturbating," the priest heard the father say.

"That's only normal," the priest replied, almost without thinking, and blushing a little. He hadn't expected such a confession. In the end, he looked away and kept his eyes fixed on the carts laden with wood.

"Not in a three-year-old. If, as you say, he is just a big child, he wouldn't masturbate. And I'm really worried. I can't sleep for thinking about what might happen."

"Nothing will happen," the priest said without much conviction. Now he too was worried.

"We don't know that. We don't know what will happen when Daniel starts to take an interest in women."

The boys' father fell silent. He was wondering whether or not to mention what was on his mind at that moment.

"When she was young, my wife Sara knew a boy like Daniel. He was the son of some farmers who lived in the same village as her. When he was the age my son is now, he started prowling around the houses of women who lived on their own. Then, a little later, he started walking about entirely naked. In the end, he attacked a girl coming home from a fiesta. That same year, he turned up drowned in the river."

"You mean they killed him?" asked the priest, unable to disguise the tremor in his voice.

"Of course," said the father.

"And why didn't they put him in an asylum before things got that far?" the priest exclaimed, trying to suppress his own fear. "Anyway Daniel will never follow that path. He may respond to certain bodily needs, because nature demands it, but he will never connect those needs with the women he sees around him. In that respect, he is a three-year-old, a child. And like all children, he sees a woman as two things only, as mother or playmate."

Even he didn't believe what he was saying. It was merely a way of trying to avoid the problem. No, his words gave no real indication as to where the crux of the matter lay. Yet he felt incapable of going any deeper than that because he was afraid of everything to do with that crux: he feared words like "masturbation", he feared the fluids that emerged from the secret orifices of the body, he feared women's bodies, and, above

23

all, the part that his teachers at the seminary referred to as *verenda mulieris*. Besides, the area of his mind that stored all these fears stored many others too, all the fears that a weak nature such as his could not screen out or block, and that area was, so to speak, about to collapse under the weight of its shameful load. No, he could not risk stirring things up, and there was no room to store anything else. He had to change the subject. When one of the workers came over to them to say that the wood had all been loaded, he breathed a sigh of relief. This was his chance.

"Where are you taking the wood?" he asked.

"To the station," said the father of the two brothers.

"It's lucky they built the station only a couple of miles from Obaba. That should help your business."

"My sons love the trains," the man went on, ignoring the priest's remark. "They'll be angry with me when they find out we've been down there with the wood, especially Daniel, because that's one thing he does understand. The workers just have to start loading up, and he comes racing down from the house to sit on one of the carts. And you should see him at the station. As soon as the engine appears, he starts shrieking with excitement."

"It's still best that he goes to school with his brother. Even if he doesn't learn anything, at least he'll get used to being with other people. And the same goes for the other children. They'll get used to him and gradually come to accept him."

"I hope so," said the father. A moment later, both he and everything surrounding him – the sawmill, the logs, the piles of planks – had vanished from the mind of the man in black, and in its place was the image of a road running between green

24

hills. I suddenly saw Paulo and Daniel, walking along hand in hand, and I saw the man in black too, walking in the opposite direction to the two brothers.

"Where are you off to?" the man asked when they met.

"To the station, Father," replied Paulo.

"And you're walking all the way?"

"It's not that far for us," said Paulo. He seemed rather troubled by these questions.

"I like the train," said Daniel, bursting out laughing.

"But why are you going there on your own? Why don't you go with the other boys?"

"The others make fun of Daniel," said Paulo firmly, but without looking up.

The thoughts of the man in black were growing ever slower; they moved like a dying fish allowing itself to be carried this way and that, and which might be sucked into a whirlpool or simply stop and sink to the bottom. Thus – after the conversation on the road – I saw images of cherries, of children playing or sitting at their desks, of girls walking along the streets of Obaba or along the road, and of Paulo, Daniel and ejaculations. But mostly of girls and ejaculations.

Then, after a time, all the images came to a halt.

"He's gone to sleep," I thought. And it was true.

# THE SQUIRRELS' STORY

*How we recognised Daniel.*
*The girls with the cakes*

WE SQUIRRELS USED TO live by the stream, in a place full of hazel trees, and we never lacked for anything, neither food nor water nor places to sleep, and for that reason we thought we would stay there for ever. But just as summer was beginning, we heard a voice inside us, and it ordered us to go somewhere else.

"Can you hear me?" said the voice.

"Well, I certainly can," I replied.

"So can I," said the squirrel beside me.

"Perfectly," said the third squirrel.

"We can hear you too," said the other three.

The voice inside us went on to say:

"This is what I want you to do. You must go at once and find the boy with almost nothing in his head. Find him quickly; a little tune will guide you."

"What tune?" we asked.

"Of all the many things one can have in one's head, that tune is all he has in his. That is the tune you will hear."

And so it was. As soon as the voice disappeared, we heard

the notes of a melody, do do mi mi mi mi fa so fa mi so so fa mi
re fa fa mi fa so, and we all set off to find where it was coming
from. We couldn't always hear the melody clearly, for sometimes
it went very quiet and even stopped altogether, but in the end we
always found it again – that opening do do mi mi mi – and
this really reassured us, in fact we would have liked the melody
to go on for ever.

At first, we headed upstream, but the further we went in that
direction, the weaker the melody seemed to become. I turned to
the other squirrels and I said:

"The boy with almost nothing in his head doesn't live in this
direction. He lives down there."

Since no one disagreed with me, we turned round and went
towards the valley, towards Obaba.

"You see?" I said shortly afterwards. "We can hear the melody
much more clearly now. If we continue in this direction, we'll
soon reach the boy's house."

At last, we reached a spot near a sawmill, and you could hear
the melody ever so clearly, but there was a problem: there were
a lot of houses nearby and it was very hard to know which of
the houses the melody was coming from; we didn't know what
to think, was it coming from that house or wasn't it, do you
think it's this one or that one, and since we couldn't decide, we
thought it would be best if we each went off in a different
direction, six different directions in all.

"Then we'll meet back here," I said.

"But what if we get lost?" said one squirrel.

"We won't get lost," I said to reassure her. "I don't think we'll
have to go very far to find where the melody is coming from."

So we all set off on our own. I went as far as the village square and there I stayed, asking myself questions and answering them: Does the boy live in one of these stone houses? No, obviously not; since the melody is fainter here than it was near the sawmill, I'll have to go back. After a while, I rejoined the other squirrels.

"Well, he isn't down by the square," I told them.

Four squirrels said the same, that he wasn't in any of the places they had explored. However, the last one pointed to the hill just above the sawmill and said that on the top of the hill was a house with many windows and that up there the melody was really loud.

"So that's where the boy must live," I said.

We got into a line and set off along the road that led from the sawmill up to the house. There was no need to listen hard for the tune, do do mi mi mi mi fa so fa mi so so fa mi re fa fa mi fa so; on the contrary, it was so loud we couldn't hear anything else. When we got near to the house, we climbed into the branches of an apple tree and started discussing what we should do.

"Look," I said, "there's an open window. We'd better just go inside."

The other squirrels agreed, and we soon found ourselves in a room containing a very large bed covered by a maroon coun-terpane, on top of which was a piece of stale bread. Then we remembered that we had had no food since we first started looking for the boy with almost nothing in his head and so we started eating. You could hear the melody so clearly in that room it made us all slightly drunk.

Suddenly, when we were least expecting it, two boys appeared in the doorway, one big and fat and the other one smaller, and we immediately forgot about the bread and sat there, alert, wondering which was the boy with almost nothing in his head, the one we had to find.

"Squirrels, Paulo," said the big boy, and we all thought, that's him, that's the boy with almost nothing in his head, and we were really glad, and he must have been glad too because he came over to the bed, laughing. And we were thrilled when he picked us up in his arms. We were completely drunk on the melody. We felt so good that we didn't even miss what we had left behind, the stream, the hazel trees and everything.

"Of course you can play, Daniel," said the other boy, and we thought, so his name is Daniel, good, we'll stay with Daniel for ever and we'll listen to his tune all day and all night.

"We've been very lucky," said one of the squirrels.

And, of course, we all agreed, because that night none of us suspected what was going to happen, and anyway, at first, events seemed to prove us right because we spent the time in the attic, the six of us and Daniel, and it was marvellous to hear those notes repeated over and over, do do mi mi mi mi fa so fa mi so so fa mi re fa fa mi fa so. Daniel seemed happy too, he kept laughing loudly and brought us walnuts and hazelnuts and got very annoyed when his brother called him, Daniel, come down to supper this minute, and he said, no, Paulo, I don't want to come down, but it was no use, his brother was always giving him orders or taking him off with him somewhere, sometimes to supper, sometimes to the sawmill and at others to the station. His brother couldn't understand, he didn't want Daniel and us to be together, and he didn't want us to leave the attic either, because when we did and got into one of the bedrooms, he

32

would threaten us with a stick and order an old woman to drive us back up to the attic. Not that we were unhappy, at least not as unhappy as we are now, because we knew that at some time of day or night Daniel would come back to see us.

Many days passed and the summer heat became more intense, especially in the attic where we were living, and because we were always thirsty, Daniel brought us a bucket of water every day, which was fine, but things weren't really fine, because with the heat we began to lose our appetite and to grow weak. For his part, Daniel was always sweating and he was getting tired of playing with us and, on some days, he didn't even come up to see us at all.

We couldn't possibly go on like that and so we slipped through the grille covering one of the small attic windows and went to live in the apple tree next to the house. From there we could still hear Daniel's tune, and we were less affected by the heat.

One night, I woke up suddenly and I sensed that something strange was happening. I soon realised what it was. I could hear the tune only very faintly and weakly.

"I don't know about you, but I can hardly hear Daniel. I don't think he's in the house."

When they listened carefully, the others all agreed. It was the same for them too.

"I think he's left the house. Yes, that's it, while we were sleeping, Daniel left the house," I said.

"In this heat?" said one of the squirrels.

"At night and with no light?" said another.

"Wasn't he supposed to come and see us?" said the others.

"Indeed he was," I said, "but the fact is he didn't, and the tune is getting fainter and fainter. If we don't hurry up and follow him, we might lose him for ever. We'd better go and look for him."

But none of us moved from the branch we were on because we felt so lethargic, not quite as much as we do now, but pretty lethargic nonetheless.

"Come on," I managed to say at last, because I was sure it was our duty to go. "Let's find Daniel as quickly as possible."

I managed to get the other squirrels moving, and we set off down the hill. Then, leaving the sawmill behind us, we started walking along a path that followed the river and crossed many meadows full of grass, which looked black in the darkness, and we continued in that direction because that is what the tune told us to do, because the notes of the song were growing stronger and stronger, do do mi mi mi mi fa so fa mi so so fa mi re fa fa mi fa so. When we had been walking for some time, our ears told us we should turn off towards the road that went down the valley and followed the river, just as the path did, only on the other side. Soon we were once more engulfed by the tune, and there was Daniel sitting on a wall by the side of the road. And he wasn't alone. There were some other boys with him, and they were all silent and intent, all of them watching one of the bends in the road, waiting for something to appear, and so we did the same, we joined the group and waited for something to appear.

Seven girls appeared, each of them mounted on a bike. First, we saw a bicycle light, then another and, shortly after that, three lights together and, finally, two lights, and as the bicycles approached, the girls' bodies began to take shape, and the smell grew more intense, because that was the thing we were most aware of, the wonderful smell those girls brought with them, and it turned out that they came laden with cakes and pies.

"What's going on?" we wondered, when we saw Daniel and the other boys on the wall get up and start whooping with joy. Then we found out, because the voice told us, that the girls all went to the village-with-the-railway-station in order to learn how to make cakes and that the cakes and pies they had made they shared out amongst the boys from Obaba who came to meet them.

When the girls got nearer, they started ringing their bells and turning their bicycle lights off and on, and the boys started whooping so loudly that the birds sleeping in the trees nearby were frightened, and we were too – a bit.

"Cake!" screamed Daniel, going over to the two girls at the rear of the group. One of them had long, yellow hair, the other long, black hair.

"Give him some of yours, Carmen. Mine didn't turn out very well today. I put too much sugar in them," said the girl with yellow hair. Meanwhile, Daniel held out his hands, laughing, his mouth wide.

"What difference does it make, Teresa? Fatty here won't notice the difference anyway," said the other girl sourly.

"What a way to talk about your cousin!" said Teresa. She had a nice laugh.

"It's awful having someone like him in the family," said Carmen in her sour voice. "He disgusts me."

"You shouldn't talk like that. I hate to think what would happen if Paulo heard you," said Teresa.

"Oh, I was forgetting, you're keen on Paulo, aren't you?" laughed Carmen. Her laugh was sour too. "Well, I'll have you know that I like Paulo too. He's rather dishy."

"Be quiet, Carmen! Can't you see Daniel is listening?"

"So what! Fatty here doesn't understand anything. Isn't that right, Daniel? You don't understand what's wrong with Teresa, do you?"

Daniel stood open-mouthed. Then he looked at the basket strapped onto the carrier on Teresa's bike.

"Cake, Teresa!" he said.

"All right, Daniel, I'll give you some cake. But it's much too sugary," said Teresa, releasing the elasticated band securing the basket. "Just don't tell Paulo I gave it to you," she added.

"You liar, Teresa. You want Paulo to find out the truth," said Carmen, sniggering. Then she gave Daniel a shove. "Go on, off you go. Go home and tell Paulo all about it, if you can! Could you, Daniel? Do you think you could? Of course you couldn't. You'll probably gobble down all the cakes before you get home anyway."

What happened that night was repeated many times. Daniel would go down to the road to wait for the two girls, Carmen and Teresa, and Carmen would speak to him scornfully and Teresa would give him cakes and, after that, we would all go home. But suddenly, when we least expected it, when we were getting used to those nocturnal expeditions, everything changed. The worst thing that could possibly happen happened, the tune disappeared from Daniel's head.

It was on one of those expeditions. That night Teresa was wearing a very thin white blouse that emphasised her breasts, and as she was about to give Daniel the cake, she accidentally brushed against his arm with one of her breasts. Daniel felt a tremor, a tremor that ran down the length of his spine and that made him grab hold of Teresa and slightly lift up her skirt, and at that moment, Teresa let out a soft cry, and Carmen hit Daniel over the head with her bicycle pump, crying out like Teresa, only much more loudly.

"You horrible, disgusting pig!" yelled Carmen. Daniel burst into tears, and the tune suddenly vanished.

"Don't shout at him like that, Carmen. He doesn't know what he's doing," said Teresa, rather frightened by her friend's anger.

"Of course he does! It isn't the first time he's tried it on with a girl!" shouted Carmen, her voice sourer than ever. She hated Daniel. "They should lock him up!"

Daniel was whimpering. And the tune in his head still did not come back.

"He didn't do anything to me. Leave him alone," said Teresa.

"What would he have to do to you, then, pull down your knickers?"

"Oh, shut up!" said Teresa.

"Oh, I get it, this is all for Paulo's sake! That's why you're so nice to Daniel! Fine, I'll leave you to it, then!"

Carmen got on her bike and disappeared. Despite the stars in the sky, it was very dark, and we could barely make out the only two people left on that part of the road, Teresa and Daniel.

"Please, stop crying. You can't stay here crying all night," said Teresa when she saw that Daniel was still snivelling. His only response was to reach out his hand to her breasts.

"Look, if you stop crying, I'll let you touch me," she said, leaving the road and going behind a tree.

Daniel stopped crying at once. Perhaps the tune will come back into his head now, I thought. But it didn't.

"But just this once, all right, just this once!" said Teresa unbuttoning her blouse and leaving her breasts bare. They were round and very white. Daniel again felt the tremor run down his spine. Then he started panting and laughing.

Several days have passed since then and our situation goes from bad to worse. Daniel leaves the house at all hours of the day and night, and the other squirrels ask me where our big friend has gone and when he'll be coming back, and I have to tell them I don't know, he's not like he used to be, the tune has vanished from his head, and we'll never hear those notes again, do do mi mi mi mi fa so fa mi so so fa mi re fa fa mi fa so, and I'm really worried and so is everyone else in the house, at least his brother Paulo is, and on the other hand, no one spares a thought for us squirrels any more, no one brings hazel‑nuts and walnuts up to us in the attic, no water either, and that's how things are now, really bad, especially with this heat, and that's why I ask the voice every day to free us from our obligation to follow Daniel and to allow us to go back to the hazel tree next to the stream, where we will never lack for water or food.

# THE BIRD TAKES UP
# THE STORY AGAIN

*Paulo's life. A conversation with Carmen.*
*Teresa's love*

AFTER HIS FATHER'S FUNERAL, Paulo went back to what had become his normal life since he left school to work at the sawmill. He got up very early, before seven, and worked the mechanical saw until, at around eleven, the workers called him to go with them to the guesthouse in the square where they all had a mid-morning snack. After the break, they would work until two, when Paulo would go up to the house to have lunch with Daniel. By four, he was back at the sawmill and he would stay there until the church bells rang out sadly, indicating that the shadows of night were already present in the sky over Obaba.

However, although Paulo's life continued exactly as it had in the previous months, something had changed. Now he woke alone, with no one to knock on his bedroom door to tell him it was time to get up, and, shortly afterwards, when he went down the hill or went over to the mechanical saw, he thought he could see a void, a kind of man made of smoke or air, who moved just as his father used to move. But these changes and strange presences did not upset him. He managed to overcome his fear and to appear, as he always had, a calm, serious lad of few words.

41

As for me, I used to hang around the sawmill, flying about amongst the alder trees along the river or going as far as the hut where the workmen changed their clothes. But I could go no further, however much I wanted to. The sawdust choked me and prevented me from getting any nearer to Paulo. Only at night did I manage to get close to him, while he was having supper or resting in his room. I say resting, because he slept very little, only between four and half past six in the morning, more or less.

After a few weeks, the apparent normality, Paulo's silence and the customary calm of Obaba began to worry me. Despite its being the hottest part of the summer, there were times when I felt cold.

"Something bad is going to happen," I would think then. Nevertheless, I tried to avoid such thoughts by concentrating on other things, for example by watching the apples that were carried along by the river, as they were every summer. I would watch them bobbing about as they tumbled over the little waterfalls, then disappeared beneath the surface only to re-emerge amongst the foam and be spun round by the whirling water, until, at last, they were swept downstream, under the bridge and out towards the sea. That movement of water and apples kept me amused. But did it stop me thinking dark thoughts? Not always. Almost without my realising it, the image of Paulo would resurface in my mind. I would see him walking like a man, working like a man, talking to his monstrous brother like a man, but suffering with a heart that was not yet a man's heart and which could barely cope with the burden his father's death had bequeathed to him. Then I would feel cold again.

The apples in the river were green at first, small apples

that had been torn from the branches as soon as they appeared amongst the leaves and hurled into the water. Later, others appeared, yellow or reddish, that got bruised on the rocks and dissolved in the water. Yes, time was passing, the summer was reaching its peak. Around the river, the fields of corn were building walls of an even intenser green than the grass. In the gardens beside the houses in Obaba, the tomatoes had grown fat and red.

Paulo liked those fat, red tomatoes and ate them every day while he joked with Daniel or chatted with the old woman who did the household chores about the latest news in Obaba or about some incident at the sawmill. Then everything in the house seemed normal, as if life were following a route as fixed and sure as that followed by the train the two brothers so loved to watch. Paulo seemed to be recovering rapidly from the loss of his father; Daniel was happy playing with his squirrels. But I knew this apparent calm was false. Paulo still had trouble sleeping and, as time passed, the situation grew worse, and his nights became filled with unpleasant thoughts in which Sara, the woman who had been his mother, almost always figured. She would talk to him of things I knew nothing about, and then she would start crying and telling him to be careful and not to trust Daniel or his father's brother, Uncle Antonio.

"Listen to your mother, Paulo," his mother would say inside his head. She was a white-haired lady, almost as old as the old woman who did the household chores, only rather more elegant. "Don't trust your Uncle Antonio. He wants to get control of the sawmill. But the sawmill is yours. First, it was mine, then it belonged to your father and me, because your father worked so hard there, but in future it should be yours alone. Do you hear me, Paulo?"

"Yes, mother," Paulo would say in a childish voice.

"That's why I don't want you going to Uncle Antonio's house. There's no reason why you should be friends with your cousin Carmen. Have whatever other friends and girlfriends you choose, but if you want my opinion, I would rather you married the poorest girl in Obaba than Carmen."

"Yes, mother," Paulo would say again in that same childish voice. "If Uncle Antonio comes to the sawmill, I won't let him in."

When the person who appeared in his thoughts was his father, Paulo would hear again the words he had said to him at the hour of his death, take care of Daniel, he's not just a piece of old rag, you must watch over him, and then Paulo would get up and go to his brother's bedroom to see how he was. Usually, Daniel was fine, fast asleep, but despite that, Paulo would look in on him at least twice every night.

I don't know how many nights this went on. Many nights. Paulo was getting wearier and weaker all the time and he had dark shadows under his eyes.

"What can I do to help him?" I would think.

One day, almost unwittingly, I found a way. One night, I flew closer than usual to his bed, and Paulo saw me. He obviously found it so odd that a bird should be in his bedroom that he forgot to think, he forgot to listen to the voices of his father and mother. Shortly afterwards – I kept flying about all the time – he was asleep. After that, I did the same thing every night. And Paulo's health improved. He slept well and only thought

44

about Daniel when he woke up. Then he would go into Daniel's room and sit on the bed.

"What's wrong, Paulo?" Daniel would ask when he saw him there.

"Are you all right?" Paulo would ask.

"Yes, I'm fine."

And there the conversation ended, because Daniel would fall asleep again. The truth is that his monstrous brother had a better life than Paulo. He spent all day playing with the children in the square or building castles or making designs out of the piles of sawdust in the mill or having fun with the squirrels in the attic. And Paulo was not the only one to take an interest in Daniel's fate; the old woman who did the household chores tried to keep him happy too. She would leave sweets for him in one or more corners of the house. Daniel never knew she did this.

"The squirrels leave them, Paulo," Daniel would say.

"Aren't you lucky getting sweets every day! Now you really will get fat!"

Daniel only had to hear those words to burst into wild laughter.

"He is a monster," I thought, "but an innocent monster."

I was wrong. Soon after that, Daniel changed. He acquired new habits, among them that of sneaking out of the house in the evening and staying out until late into the night.

"Where does he go?" I wondered. I felt uneasy.

Some time later, one moonlit night, Paulo realised what was happening and he was even more worried about it than I was. He went over in his mind all the places where his brother might go – the sawmill, the square in Obaba, the river – and then

45

he ran down the hill. Most of the time he spent searching the banks of the river. He even thought Daniel might have drowned.

But he hadn't drowned, far from it. Daniel calmly returned home and, with unexpected guile, slipped silently into his room.

"Where have you been?" Paulo asked him, coming out into the corridor and catching him unawares.

Daniel scowled at him as if to say: "Go away, leave me alone, you're not my keeper." Then he went into his room and slammed the door. Paulo stayed out in the corridor, not daring to go after him. He felt bewildered. He no longer had any authority over Daniel. Or worse, the trust that had always existed between them had abruptly disappeared with that slammed door.

Daniel's behaviour became odder and odder. He lost all interest in the squirrels or the children who used to play with him in the square, and he wanted nothing to do with Paulo. All he wanted was to go out and be near Teresa, the girl who gave him cakes. That was why he went down to the road every night or, during the day, to the sewing class where the girl was learning to sew.

"Can I come with you?" Paulo asked him once.

"No, you can't," replied his brother, moving his head from side to side like an ox.

The voices that Paulo used to hear at night, the voices of his mother and his father, became shrill, urgent, relentless.

"Listen, Paulo, listen," Sara, his mother, would say to him. "Watch your brother, watch him closely, because your brother is like an animal. Haven't you noticed how he likes to go around naked? And what about his hand? Haven't you noticed where he usually has his hand? Between his legs, Paulo. He's always touching himself. He has no soul, Paulo, he's a monster."

"Take care of him, Paulo, take care of him," his father would say. "Don't take any notice of what Sara tells you. She's ill. She's suffered with her nerves ever since you were both small, and she often says things she shouldn't. She says Daniel is an animal and that he should be locked up, but it's not true. He's not a bad boy. And it's your duty to take care of him. Take care of him, Paulo, take care of him."

"Your father is a good man, but he's afraid to face up to reality. If you don't keep a close watch on Daniel, you'll be sorry. And the same goes for Uncle Antonio, although for different reasons."

Paulo tossed and turned in bed, frightened by what he heard, more frightened still when he associated those words with his brother's changed behaviour.

One night, he heard noises coming from the room next door and decided to get up and investigate. What he wanted was to recover the trust that had existed between them until only recently. However, an unpleasant surprise awaited him on the other side of the door. Daniel was lying naked on the bed, and the fair hair on his belly and his pubis was covered in a thick, sticky liquid.

Without quite knowing why, Paulo went over to the wardrobe to the right of the door.

"Mine!" Daniel shouted, getting up from the bed and shoving Paulo aside.

"Why did you do that?" shouted Paulo, who had been thrown to the floor.

"Mine!" shouted Daniel again, opening the wardrobe door and removing a cake. It was a chocolate cake.

47

"Why did you have to push me so hard? You hurt me!" yelled Paulo furiously, not even noticing the cake. He raised one hand to his shoulder.

"It's mine! It's mine! It's mine!" said Daniel over and over. At that moment, naked and squealing, he did look exactly like a pig.

I suddenly felt ill and decided to escape from that house. I found the window and flew off into the night.

I don't know how long I was away from the house. I only know that in my flight I saw woods and mountains I had never seen before, and that, in the end, worn out, I returned to the tree by the stream. I hoped to find the other birds in my flock there, but the tree was empty. Empty and silent.

"Go back," I heard someone say. It was the voice again. And, as always, it seemed to emerge both from the silence and from inside me.

Just as on that first occasion, I flew down the valley until the stream became as wide and deep as a river and then I flew on over the alder trees until I reached the sawmill. Since I couldn't see Paulo – the mechanical saw was silent – I went up to the house.

The atmosphere there seemed strange to me. The squirrels looked ill and were huddled in the attic, and the guard dog, lying outside his kennel, seemed oblivious to everything going on around him. As for the old woman who did the household chores, she was sitting in the kitchen, doing nothing.

"Where can Paulo be?" I thought. Then I remembered the cake that had appeared in the wardrobe in Daniel's room and the road that linked Obaba with the village-with-the-railway-station, and the girls who brought back cakes on their bicycles.

"Paulo has gone after Daniel," I thought.

It was getting dark when I set off after him. There were a few stars in the sky, and the heat of the earth – or, rather, the heat the earth gave off after a day of sun – filled the air with mist. Despite that, it wasn't hard to make out the ten or so bicycle lights on the road.

"The girls," I said to myself.

I found Paulo at once. He was leaning on a milestone by the road watching his brother, who was standing further on round a bend, surrounded by other boys. Soon afterwards, the girls approached ringing their bicycle bells, and all the boys started whooping with delight.

"He's a pig," I thought when I saw Daniel push his way past them. The smell of cakes and pies filled the air. "There's that noise in Paulo's head again," I thought. The noise was none other than the shrill, urgent, relentless voices of his mother and his father. The two of them were shouting at the boy inside his head.

"Mine!" yelled Daniel.

"I wonder which girl gives Daniel the cakes?" I thought.

The lamp on one of the bicycles lit up again. Someone was pedalling towards Paulo.

"Would you like one?" said the girl, stopping alongside him and offering him a cake. She had a slightly sour voice.

Paulo's thoughts went back to the days before his mother's death, and he saw a house, not his, but a smaller one near a bridge, and he saw himself when he was about seven years old, accompanied by a little girl, and they were making a dam of stones in a pool in the river. Before the image disappeared from his head, a man wearing a hat was taking a photograph of the dam, with him and the little girl sitting on the same stone. I knew

49

that the man in the hat was Uncle Antonio and that the little girl, his daughter, was Carmen, the same girl who had just stopped by Paulo's side.

"Oh, it's you," Paulo said to the girl, not even looking at the cake she was holding out to him.

"Who would you like it to be?" said the girl, putting the cake back into the bag hanging from the handlebars. Her voice was still slightly sour, but it had a mocking edge to it now.

Paulo was not in the mood for jokes. He simply wanted to know the name of the girl who was giving cakes to his brother, and then go home.

"What's all this ruckus?" he asked. He was very serious.

"It's not a ruckus, it's a party," the girl replied. "We make the boys happy and ask for nothing in return. For your information, we're turning into excellent pastry cooks," she added affectedly, as if imitating someone else.

"Well, you're causing me a lot of problems," said Paulo.

"Causing you problems? And how exactly are we doing that?" laughed the girl.

"You know perfectly well."

"No, I don't actually."

Paulo was getting more and more agitated. He glanced towards the bend in the road – the boys had stopped whooping now – and breathed out slowly.

"Who is it who gives Daniel cakes? Is it you, Carmen?"

"Me? To that fatso? You must be mad!" And the girl laughed again.

"Well, go away then. I don't feel like talking to you," said Paulo, his lips tightening. His heart was thudding in his chest.

"Poor old Paulo! You have had bad luck!" said the girl. She seemed to be pitying him. Or mocking him. Before he had time to reply, the other girls rode past ringing their bells and waving cheerfully. After them came the boys, most of them eating a cake or a piece of pie.

"My poor cousin," Carmen went on, placing one foot on her bicycle pedal. Paulo's silence seemed to embolden her. "There's no reason why I should tell you anything, because you don't deserve it, but I'm going to anyway. People are saying unkind things about you, Paulo. They don't understand that mania of yours for staying at home and not talking to anyone. Or, rather, they do understand it, too well really, because they think it's out of pride, not out of love for your poor brother. So take some advice from a member of your own family, Paulo. You've got to change. You've got to let us all take responsibility for Daniel and share the load between us. If you don't, people will think you've turned out like Aunt Sara, who always acted as if she was royalty and despised everyone."

Paulo remained silent and motionless. Despite the stars the night was very black.

"This girl is a serpent," I thought. She had deliberately adopted a more persuasive tone of voice.

"I'll tell you something else too," Carmen went on, speaking more softly and weighing every word. "There are still people in the village who think well of you, but if you go on the way you are now, even they will give up on you. You don't want them to wait in vain, do you? Of course, you'd have to make a bit of an effort too."

"Have you said everything you had to say?"

Paulo was serious, but he was upset too. He had just remembered the question he had asked his father shortly after his mother died.

"Carmen told me that now we've got no mother, she and her family will come and live with us and look after us really well. Is that true, father?"

In that memory, Paulo was barely ten years old.

"No, my dear. Carmen won't come to our house and neither will your aunt and uncle," his father had replied. He was wearing a white shirt and a black V-necked sweater. "I promised Sara. She thought they were only interested in our money, not in your or Daniel's well-being. Anyway, don't worry. We'll get a woman in to do the household chores and we'll manage."

Carmen pushed the pedals backwards, making the chain whir.

"What about you? Have you said everything you had to say?" she said, raising her voice.

"She really is arrogant," I thought.

"Oh, just get out of my sight."

Paulo expressed himself confidently, but inside things were less clear. Carmen rather frightened him.

"Nothing would give me greater pleasure," she said. Then she cycled very slowly towards the village, pedalling unenthusiastically.

Before setting off home, Paulo looked towards the bend in the road in search of his brother. Despite the darkness, he thought he could see someone. Was it Daniel? No, it wasn't, it was one of the girls with the cakes. She seemed to have got left behind. Suddenly the light on her bicycle lit up, and she came nearer.

"Hi, Paulo," she said as she passed. I thought she was going to stop, but she didn't.

"Hi, Teresa," said Paulo.

"I'd like to know who that girl is," I thought. There was something about her voice. Then I learned that she was the one who gave cakes and pies to Daniel, and that she gave them to him because of Paulo, because she was in love with him.

"Of course," I thought, "they're both adolescents." Then, as if driven by some impulse, I flew after her. That infatuation seemed to me a good thing, something that Paulo needed in order to forget his parents and all they had said to him before dying.

When I caught up with her, I had a pleasant surprise. I could listen in to Teresa's thoughts as easily as I could to Paulo's. Thus I discovered that, for more than a year now, she had been unable to get him out of her head. Sometimes she tried to forget him, but it was no use, because no sooner had she made that decision than she would bump into him everywhere, outside the sewing class, for example, or going into church or walking with Daniel to the station. However, so to speak, the worst was yet to come, for she experienced an irresistible urge to talk about him, and that made her the butt of many jokes, especially from Carmen.

"Do you know what I heard on the radio the other day?" her friend said to her. "Apparently, in Greek the word for someone with only one idea in their head is 'idiot'. So you'd better watch out, because lately you've been pretty idiotic."

"What do you mean?" Teresa protested.

"I'm only joking. But it's best you should know. Lately, all you talk about is Paulo. You're in love."

"No. I'm not."

But – at least to herself – she ended up accepting that she was. She really liked him, and the feeling explained many things, amongst them the sadness she so often felt. The problem was that Paulo led a very reclusive life and, as her friends told her, being in love with him was much the same as being in love with one of those boys who left Obaba to go off and work in California or Idaho. That, of course, was an exaggeration because she did at least see him, often, here and there, but only ever briefly, in passing, and never, for example, at the Sunday dance or at the fiestas held in Obaba. Once, with Carmen's help, she had taken all her girlfriends and gone for a walk near Paulo's house, but all she had succeeded in doing was to get him to come to the window and wave. What she wanted was to be invited in and to spend the afternoon chatting, but there was some ill feeling between Carmen's family and Paulo's, some family quarrel, and so it was impossible to meet him that way either. On walks like that, she would pick up a bit of moss or a fallen fruit, and then keep it on her bedside table, as a souvenir, but a souvenir of almost nothing, of a pair of blue eyes glancing rapidly in her direction and two thin lips greeting her with a "Hi, Teresa."

These were Teresa's thoughts as she reached the village square. The first thing she saw there was Carmen sitting on a stone bench, and so she went over to her.

"It's time to go back," I thought. I flew over their heads and back to Paulo's house. Up in the sky, the number of stars had greatly increased. Now there were thousands and thousands of them.

"It will be hot tomorrow," I thought as I slipped into the house.

# THE STAR'S STORY

*An informal chat between two girls*

IT WAS A GOOD night for sitting and chatting on the stone bench, largely because of us – myself and my fellow stars – who almost completely filled the Obaba sky; but the two girls still had some way to go before they reached home and so they walked on, wheeling their bicycles.

"What did he say to you?" asked Teresa rather anxiously.

"Say to me? What would *he* have to say to me? I told him a few home truths!" replied Carmen, who seemed angry.

Teresa felt uneasy about the pies and cakes she gave to Daniel. She didn't know if that backward boy obeyed the instructions she gave him: "Don't say anything to Paulo because, if you do, I won't give you any more cakes," and worse, she feared that as well as mentioning the cakes – which were, after all, hardly important – he might have told Paulo what had happened on the night when he wouldn't stop crying and she had let him touch her breasts. Had she done wrong? She didn't think so, since her intention had only been to put an end to another's suffering, which was what they were always telling you to do at school and at church; but she wasn't entirely sure because the contact of Daniel's great hands on her breasts had given her a shiver of pleasure, a feeling she relived almost every night in bed, only changing the actors, imagining that it was Paulo not Daniel who was touching and caressing her. The doubt had been stirring inside her for several weeks, and now – as she walked home in the company of Carmen – all that was left was its nucleus, the only thing that had mattered to her right from the start: what would Paulo think if he found out? She didn't care if the teacher or the priest in Obaba tried to shame her, just as she cared little about what her friends might think; but the possibility that Paulo might reject her because of it filled her with terror. How could she carry on after such a rejection? How could she go on living? Because as long as there was still a possibility – the possibility that he liked her – life continued to be bearable. She preferred to imagine that he did, that one day they would lie naked in the same bed, and with that hope she lightened the weight of the worst days, of winter days in Obaba, days without sun and nights without stars.

"You're not listening to me, Teresa. What are you thinking about?" Carmen said after telling her about her conversation with Paulo.

"No, I heard almost everything you said. I'm sorry. I'm a bit preoccupied," said Teresa. They had left behind them the streets of Obaba and were walking on a path that ran by the riverside.

"What about?"

"Daniel. I'm worried about Daniel. He won't leave me alone. Before, he was just after my cakes. Now it's me he's after, all the time. You've seen what happens when we're at the sewing class."

The shop where the class was held had one window that

gave onto the street. Daniel used to lean on the windowsill and stay there nearly all afternoon looking at the girls who went there to learn sewing. He looked at her most of all.

"I shouldn't worry about it, just think what you might be able to get out of your relationship with Daniel," said Carmen with a mischievous smile.

"You mean his relationship with me, don't you?"

"Yes, but don't be such a nitpicker. You know what I mean. Daniel could be a way of getting closer to Paulo. Imagine, for example, that we invited him into the shop. Then what would happen? Well, no one knows, but one thing is sure, Fatso would want to stay there for good, because though he may be stupid, he likes the girls more than any other man in Obaba. And, of course, when that happens, someone will have to go and tell Paulo what's going on, and he will have no option but to come to the shop and fetch him. That could be a real opportunity for you, Teresa, to talk to him."

"Hm, I see what you mean. It might not be a bad idea," said Teresa thoughtfully, looking up at us, the stars.

"Bear in mind that it will be the village fiesta soon. If, by then, you've managed to talk to him a couple of times, things will be easier. With a little bit of gentle persuasion, you could even get him to dance. Paulo, as you know, is one of those boys who needs encouragement."

Carmen laughed, but her laughter and her words jarred slightly.

"I doubt very much that I'll get him to do that," sighed Teresa. "At last year's fiesta he didn't even come to the dance. And this year, what with his father having died, it will be even worse. That's something I don't like about him. He's such a coward."

"It's not his fault, Teresa," said Carmen gravely. She knew her friend did not mean it, but neither did she want to lose the chance to create a climate of greater trust between them. People always demanded something in exchange for speaking about their innermost feelings, they demanded secrets in exchange for their secrets, and she was prepared to initiate that interchange, one which would, of course, be in her favour in the long run.

"Paulo is shy or, as you put it, a coward," Carmen went on, lowering her voice. "But it's all his mother's fault. You may not know this, but Aunt Sara – how can I put it? – wasn't quite right in the head, she was always in a state about things and never had a good word to say about anyone; she even spoke badly of her own family. She used to say, for example, that my father wanted to take the sawmill away from her, as if my father was a thief. Obviously, when I think about it, she wasn't to blame either. If she hadn't had a son like Daniel, she would probably have been quite normal, but she did have Daniel and she wasn't. She was quite twisted really. So you can imagine what kind of upbringing Paulo had."

"Yes, I can," said Teresa. She was deep in thought.

"Anyway, that's why Paulo is the way he is. He feels responsible for everything that happens to his brother and thinks he has to devote his whole life to him. But that's absurd. He's not a child any more, believing everything his parents told him. It's high time he grew up."

"You're right. At some point, you have to start disobeying your parents," said Teresa with conviction.

"I'll tell you something. And I mean this seriously," said Carmen, stopping and placing one hand on her shoulder. "You could do him a lot of good. Really. You could change Paulo and make him happy. Because at the moment, he isn't – not at all. You just have to look at him to know that."

"What do you mean?" asked Teresa, alarmed.

"I mean his face. He looks like someone who doesn't sleep. I'm sure he has nightmares."

"It's such a shame," sighed Teresa.

"That's why he needs you. A lot," insisted Carmen.

Teresa said nothing, thinking about Paulo, about his fair hair, blue eyes, his serious little boy's face, his shy look; and the silence at that moment surrounding the girls began to fill with the sounds of the night. A dog barked, toads were croaking somewhere along the river, and nearer, by the roadside, a cricket opened and closed its wings producing the soft noise which, when she was small, had always reminded her of a bicycle bell.

"So we'll invite Daniel into the sewing class then," Teresa said at last.

"I'll do it. You leave it to me," said Carmen. "But first I'll have to find a chair big enough for him. His great fat arse won't fit on any of the chairs we use," she added in a sour voice.

"I hope it works."

"Of course it will. You've got to get to know Paulo somehow."

"I could write him a letter," said Teresa somewhat doubtfully. It was something she had often thought about, writing to Paulo and saying: I'd really like to go out with you, I think about you day and night. I'll wait ten days for a reply and, if, after

61

that time, I hear nothing, I will try to forget you and look elsewhere. But she did not dare to be so honest. Boys were the ones who were supposed to take the initiative.

"Don't humiliate yourself by writing a letter and revealing your feelings. He'll probably just think you're easy. I honestly believe this is the best way."

"All right, we'll do as you say."

"Look, Teresa, don't be afraid. If things turn out badly, if, for example, Paulo gets angry, I'll take the blame. He'll hate me, not you."

They were getting near the hut where they kept their bikes. From there on, each would have to go her own way, Carmen to her house by the river, Teresa to hers on one of the hills around Obaba. They put their bikes away in silence, leaving them on a metal rack inside the hut.

"The thing I like most about Paulo is the way he whistles," said Teresa, still unwilling to set off towards her own house. This wasn't true, or at least it had never occurred to her until then, but the silence that had grown between them made her nervous. She was not entirely convinced by her friend's plan.

"Next you'll be saying he's an artist," laughed Carmen.

"Don Ignacio said once that very few people have Paulo's ear for music, and that he could have been a musician."

Don Ignacio was the priest in Obaba. Once, he had heard Paulo whistling Palestrina's *Magnificat* to his brother Daniel and had been genuinely impressed. Unfortunately, the boy's mother had refused to allow him to join the church choir.

"Huh, Don Ignacio! He's another one who's too clever by half!" exclaimed Carmen fiercely.

"Why do you say that?" asked Teresa, rather taken aback by her friend's tone of voice.

"Oh, take no notice of me. It's nothing."

Carmen never spoke to the priest, and a light flashed in her whenever she heard his name. He was an intelligent man, even more intelligent than her, and he was quick to see what was going on inside other people.

"Carmen, I'd like to ask you something," he had said to her once, when he met her as she was leaving the sewing class. "I'd like to know why you have two faces."

"I'm sorry, I don't know what you mean," she had said.

"Don't get angry with me, Carmen. All I mean is that you change depending on whether you're alone or with other people. When you're with someone, or in the middle of a group, you seem very arrogant, always ready to make fun of someone. But as soon as you're alone, another face appears. The face of someone so weary she can barely raise her eyes from the ground. I don't think you can go on like this. You can't go on having two faces. And if you need help, I'll make sure you get it."

"Oh, so I've got two faces, have I?" she began. Then her voice hardened. "Tell me something, Don Ignacio, which face has the birthmark?"

Carmen pointed to the enormous birthmark that covered most of her left cheek.

"That's got nothing to do with what I was saying," the priest had protested.

"Of course it does! If I have to let go of one of my faces, I'd very much like it to be the one with the birthmark!" she had laughed.

"Such things don't exist in God's eyes, Carmen. To God you're a pretty girl. And to me as well."

"What a shame everyone else doesn't think the same!"

Carmen had been unable to bear it any longer. She had suddenly started laughing like a mad thing only to burst immediately into equally wild tears. Moments later, she had run off, angry with herself for her inability to control her feelings. Ever since then, she had avoided the priest.

"What are you thinking about, Carmen?" asked Teresa.

"Oh, nothing. I was just looking at the stars," lied Carmen.

"There are so many of them," said Teresa, gazing up at them.

"I've got to get home, Teresa. I'll see you tomorrow."

"All right. When do you think you'll sort out the business with Daniel?"

"I'll think about it. Don't worry. I'll see you tomorrow."

Carmen ambled off. When she got to her house, she hesitated for a moment and then walked towards the part of the river where she used to bathe as a child and where she had her "stone seat", a square rock in the middle of the pool. It was her favourite place, the centre of the world. She always went there whenever she wanted to be alone and to think her own thoughts unseen.

# THE SNAKE'S STORY

*The words brought by the water*

I SLIPPED SLOWLY AND elegantly into the water, following to perfection the rules of deportment followed by all snakes, and I swam stealthily – for stealth too forms part of our code of conduct – towards a trout drowsing in a hollow on the river bottom. Then, just as I was about to pounce, when there were only inches between my mouth and its tail, something went wrong. I was seized by a trembling and the water around me grew agitated. My prey escaped, and I started to curse.

"Be quiet! Listen to me!" a voice inside me said. I immediately grew calm. Therein lay the cause of my ineptitude. I had not failed, the voice had made me fail. The inner voice.

"Of course," I said. "But I very much hope that one day you will compensate me for what, thanks to you, I have just lost. Nothing gives me greater pleasure than to seize a trout by the tail and then allow it to carry me along from one side of the river to the other. And the absolute peak of pleasure comes when the trout can go no further and I drag it out of the water and it suffocates. So next time . . ."

"Be quiet!" yelled the voice, interrupting me, and I closed

67

my mouth ready to receive my orders. I learned then that I was to leave the deep part of the river and swim to the surface.

"But what for?" I asked. I was still annoyed with the voice. I hate losing a prey when it is already practically mine.

"Listen to the sounds carried by the river. There are particular sounds that interest us. The words spoken by a girl, to be precise," said the voice.

"If there's no alternative, then I will, of course, listen."

I said this merely to say something, because, with the voice, there never is any alternative, and I began swimming towards the river shallows which is where most sounds accumulate. Once there, I looked around and I saw what, in the circumstances, I would prefer not to have seen, that is, I saw game, and plenty of it, I saw birds, I saw mice, I saw a beaver catching its prey, I saw twenty or so toads with their ridiculous puffed up chests, croaking foolishly, and worst of all, I saw the trout that had just given me the slip. Alas, I began to curse again.

"Be quiet and look at the girl!" the voice yelled, and just at that moment I felt a terribly painful blow to the head, as if someone had hit me with a hammer.

Half-stunned by the blow, I changed the direction of my gaze and looked beyond the delicious toads and the even more delicious trout. Then I saw the girl. She was sitting on a rock in the middle of the pool. She was holding her shoes in one hand and was stroking her cheek and chin with the other. There was a dark stain on her cheek.

"Let's see what this ugly girl is thinking about," I thought.

The current was full of hundreds of words, but most of them got lost in the noise the water made as it splashed over the stones. Besides, the girl wasn't even thinking coherently, jumping seamlessly from one thing in the past to another thing in the present and to another in the future. In the end, when I had grown bored with the little game of separating out the sounds, I heard one complete phrase.

"Tell me all the reasons why my little girl should be happy."

That was the phrase which, remembering some scene from her childhood, the girl with the dark stain on her cheek had just thought. It was, of course, nonsense, but I did not dare simply ignore her or the situation. I didn't want to annoy the voice.

The girl pondered the question. It seemed to her that at that time – during her childhood – she would have been able to find a multitude of reasons to feel happy, the first and most important being her mother's love; the second and almost equally important being her father's love; the third and also almost equally important being her cousin Paulo's love. Nevertheless – the girl was still pondering – all that belonged to the distant past. She had grown up and had realised with horror what it meant to have a birthmark on her cheek, and from that moment on it was all over for her. Especially when her cousin Paulo had let her down.

I glanced across at the trout that had eluded me. There it was, by the roots of a tree, as sound asleep as the last time I had seen it. If the girl were only kind enough to be brief, the night could still end well.

"Now's your chance to get your revenge. You can pay Paulo back for the bad turn he did to you," the girl said to herself, and the water carried away her words as if they were corks.

"Revenge is sweet," I thought.

"It's all working out really well," said the girl. Then she went on to talk about a friend of hers, Teresa, and about some cakes that they gave to Paulo's brother, a certain Daniel. Apparently these gifts were the cause of great concern to Paulo.

"Who would have thought that an animal like Daniel would be capable of having a crush on a girl," said the girl, accompanying her words with a merry laugh. "But that's what's happened. The fat pig spends hours at the window of the seamstress's shop ogling Teresa. That makes things a lot easier for me."

Her thoughts weren't bad at all, but I was beginning to grow bored. The fact is I get bored with anything that smells of waiting and delay. In my opinion, when someone wants to take revenge, they should forget all the famous theories advocating slowness and, instead, attack swiftly, violently, taking advantage of the enormous energy that comes from rage. I would have suggested this to the girl, but the voice had placed me there to listen and I had no way of communicating with her.

"Your aunt will die soon, Carmen. And when she does, then we'll all go and live in her house, you'll see. From then on, you and Paulo will be like brother and sister."

At first, I didn't understand what I was hearing, because I was still thinking about the best way to avenge oneself. However, I quickly realised that the girl – it seems her name was Carmen – was remembering something that had happened some years before, in her childhood.

"Are you sure she'll die? Are you sure we'll go and live in Paulo's house?"

"Of course I'm sure, Carmen."

After the remembered dialogue, the water was filled with complaints. The girl addressed Paulo, demanding explanations. Why hadn't he wanted her as a sister? Why hadn't he wanted them to live together? Was that pig Daniel preferable to her?

"Didn't you realise how excited I was about coming to live with you?" said the girl. The tone, of course, was deplorable, the classic tone of the weak. "You used to watch me drawing a sketch of your house and imagining which bedroom each of us would sleep in, you watched me making plans and you let me do it even though you knew my dream wouldn't come true. I'll never forgive you for that, Paulo."

"Now that's more like it," I thought.

The girl went back to her memories. The conversation she had with her mother after her aunt's death still hurt her deeply.

"We won't be going to live at your cousins' house, Carmen."

"Why not, mother?"

"It's your Aunt Sara's fault."

"But she's dead, mother."

"You're too young to understand these things, Carmen, but all I can say is that your aunt made your uncle promise some-thing. She didn't want us all to live together. And so we won't. At least not until your uncle dies too."

"And will he die soon?"

"I don't know, Carmen, but one day he will."

There was a moment of silence, then the girl gave a very strange laugh. After that, the waters brought the first interesting confession of the night.

"It seemed as if he would never die. It's just as well I helped him on his way," she said. Then she lowered her voice and became immersed in her own thoughts. As far as I could make out, she had not intended to kill her uncle. For a long time, she had wanted him to die because she associated that man's disappearance with becoming Paulo's sister, but she had wished for his death in the way that one wishes for things one knows are unobtainable. At the beginning of that summer, though, she had found herself standing outside the sawmill with a bottle of turpentine in her bag, purely by chance, because there was a piece of furniture in the sewing workshop she wanted to clean up, and then she had had the fortune or misfortune to see two things, on the one hand, a bucket of water with some ice in it and a half-empty bottle of cider, and on the other, the figure of her uncle drenched in sweat beside the mechanical saw. Suddenly, something impelled her to pour nearly the whole bottle of turpentine into the bottle of cider. Fate had then taken a hand. Before he realised anything was wrong, her uncle had drunk enough of the stuff to perforate his oesophagus and several other internal organs. Then, after a few weeks, he had died. Luckily, the police in charge of the case had made only very half-hearted investigations, and she had acquitted herself well in the interrogations, rather better than most of the other inhabitants of Obaba.

The girl fell silent, and the water filled with the sounds of the night. The wind was stirring the leaves of the alder trees. The toads were still croaking. In the distance a dog was barking.

"I didn't mean to hurt you, Paulo," the girl went on, going back to that ghastly tone of complaint. "But now I've no option but to go on hurting you. I'm lost for ever in this world and the next. Revenge is all that's left to me."

Moments later, the water again brought me the name of the other girl, Teresa. Apparently she was rather naive, and Carmen had no difficulty in leading her wherever she wanted her to go.

"How did I come to be such a false person?" she laughed.

"The important thing is to proceed with your plans. When one has to kill, one kills," I thought.

"I'm not going to kill him. I just want to make him suffer. And I'll make him suffer through Daniel," she said. It was as if she had overhead my remark. Perhaps she had, perhaps the two of us were connected by the voice.

"She's leaving," I thought as I saw her get up from the stone and walk to the edge of the river with her shoes in her hand. I turned rapidly to where I had seen the trout. My luck was in, it was still there. Free at last from my obligations, I began swimming towards it in the way we snakes do, elegantly, stealthily.

# THE BIRD TAKES UP
# THE STORY AGAIN

*A serious conversation.*
*An argument at the sewing class*

THAT SUMMER THE HEAT was suffocating, and the squirrels who had so often played with Daniel eventually died of thirst. The old woman who did the household chores swept up their little bodies and threw them into a hole dug by a tree, as if they were so much rubbish. And thus their story ended, in the worst possible way.

During that time, that is, during the time it took for the squirrels to die, Daniel was never at home. Whenever I thought about him, I would see him on the road that goes to the station, waiting for the girls with the cakes, or else at the window of the sewing workshop, on mountain paths, or near the river: he was always outside and always – and this was the great novelty – trailing after Carmen's friend, a girl called Teresa. It was not something I liked to see. Whenever I wondered how it would all end, I remembered the black fish which I had seen swimming in the sea very shortly after I first heard the voice and came to Obaba. Had that been a bad omen? I had no idea, but there were times when that image filled me with foreboding, especially when I thought about Paulo's behaviour – because Paulo seemed to be going from bad to worse. He scarcely ate anything for lunch, even less for supper, and when he went into his bedroom, he lay there for hours just waiting for his brother to come home. Lying there, he was constantly assailed by memories.

"Take care of Daniel, Paulo," his father would say again. "Take care of your brother at all times, come rain or shine, in July and all year round. I will be dead soon and you are the only one who can take on this task. Someone else can look after the sawmill, someone else can look after the house, but, without you, Daniel will have no one."

"He won't obey me, father," whispered Paulo.

"You can't just stay at home. You must take steps to control your brother," I was thinking.

At that moment, it didn't look as if things were going to change, at least that was my impression; it didn't look as if Paulo would take any action. In the end, though, he had no option. He was forced into it by Don Ignacio, which is the name of the man in black, the priest in Obaba. One day, Paulo was coming back from the sawmill and he found the man sitting outside his front door. He seemed completely oblivious to the dog's furious barking.

"Get into your kennel!" shouted Paulo. The dog stopped barking at once and obeyed.

"Please, sit down," Don Ignacio said to Paulo, indicating the stone bench outside the house. "How's work going? I see you're taking a lot of wood down to the station," he added, as Paulo sat down next to him.

"That's right. We're sending the wood to Valencia."

"I was in Valencia once. It gets just as hot there as it does

78

here," said Don Ignacio, looking up at the sun.

"So I read in the school encyclopaedia," said Paulo. He was feeling tense, waiting to find out what the man had to say to him. Fortunately, the words he was waiting for were not long in coming.

"Paulo, I have a couple of things to say to you. One is general, the other particular. And since I imagine that after a full morning's work you must be tired and hungry, I'll get straight to the point. Is that all right?"

"Fine."

"Look, Paulo, I believe that just as our eyes become accustomed to the dark, so does our soul. After a while, it forgets all about the light and comes to believe that there is nothing beyond the shadows. Even if a little light did get in, our soul would still refuse to believe in it because, at first, that light would seem blinding. Do you follow me?"

"Perfectly," said Paulo firmly. Perhaps bemused by that response, Don Ignacio hesitated slightly.

"Anyway, Paulo, that, in general terms, is what I think is happening to you. You've lived surrounded by misfortunes for so long now that you've grown used to them. You've grown so used to them that you no longer expect anything else. But that needn't necessarily be so. Luckily, you're very young and you have time on your side. As long as you don't insist on continuing to turn your back on life, you could still be very happy."

"I'll bear it in mind," said Paulo quietly. He felt embarrassed by the conversation. It was too personal.

"Fine, let's move on to the particular," said Don Ignacio, getting up and turning his back on Paulo. From that hill he could see the whole valley. "I've spoken to you up until now as I would to any young man your age, but now I must talk to you quite differently. Now I need to talk to you in your role as head of the family, as your brother's guardian."

The priest turned round and looked at him. Paulo lowered his eyes.

"As you wish," he said.

"You know what Daniel's like at the moment, don't you?" asked the priest, looking back at the valley. "Well, I'll tell you," he went on, before Paulo had time to respond. "He's completely out of control, chasing the girls and frightening them out of their wits. In fact, Teresa's mother came to see me yesterday. Daniel, it seems, has a crush on Teresa and spends all night prowling round their house like an animal on heat."

"I didn't know that. But, anyway, I don't think his intentions are bad. He's like a child," said Paulo, no longer intimidated.

"Please, Paulo, listen to me," said the priest gently. He was still looking out over the valley. "We have to face facts. It's hard, but necessary. It's every man's duty to do so and it's your duty now."

"All right. Fine," said Paulo.

"At first, I shared your view," said the priest, walking towards the kennel and then retracing his steps. "I didn't think there was any malice in Daniel; I thought that the things people told me about him were pure gossip. But after the conversation I had with Teresa's mother, I asked around and everyone agrees. Some put it more gently than others, but they all talk about your brother's sexual appetite. Do you understand, Paulo?"

"The people in Obaba have never had anything good to say about us," said Paulo.

"You shouldn't say that, because it's not true. It's not true at all. You see how you always see the negative side of things. You see how you're always looking into the shadows," said the priest, stopping his pacing back and forth and speaking more loudly. However, he immediately reverted to his conciliatory tone. "It's not too late to put things right, Paulo. If you take care of your brother and don't leave him alone, things can still be put right."

"Lately, he won't obey me," said Paulo.

"Well, make him obey you. Otherwise, I dread to think what will happen. Do you know what some people have said to me? That he should be locked up in some institution."

"Locked up? Away from Obaba?" said Paulo, getting up. His eyes were very wide.

"Better that than roaming around getting up to all kinds of disgusting things," said the priest bluntly. As before, however, he immediately changed his tone of voice. "But we haven't reached that point yet. If you can get your brother to behave normally, nothing will happen."

"All right. I'll do my best," said Paulo. He seemed tired.

"You're the only one who can do it. If he had a spark of intelligence, then I would talk to him myself. But he doesn't; he can only be reached through his feelings."

"I'll do my best," said Paulo again. "Would you like something to drink before you leave?" he asked, seeing that the priest was about to say goodbye.

"No, thank you, Paulo, I have to get back to the church. By the way, do you know where your brother is right now? He's where he was all day yesterday, at the sewing class. Apparently, no one can shift him."

"I shouldn't think he'll stay there long. He soon gets bored sitting still."

"Well, he didn't get bored yesterday, but let's just hope everything turns out all right," sighed the priest. Then he gave a wave and disappeared down the hill. He walked lightly as if the conversation had lifted a weight from his shoulders.

After lunch, Paulo went down to the sawmill and stayed there working the mechanical saw until mid-afternoon. Then he stopped the machine and indicated to the men working with him that he was leaving, that he had things to do. I wasn't surprised by this decision. The conversation he had had at midday with the priest kept going round and round in his head. Yes, he would go and find Daniel, bring him home and make him obey him.

When he dusted off his trousers with the scarf he had been wearing round his head, the specks of dust and sawdust got in his mouth and made him cough.

"Steady there, Paulo," said one of the workers, smiling.

Angry at his own clumsiness, he quickly changed his clothes and raced off. There was no sign of movement anywhere in Obaba – in the square, in the streets, in the windows of the houses. Even the river seemed to have stopped flowing; it was as if it was full of crickets not water, because there the whirring of insects seemed at its most intense, spreading out from slope to slope, to the hills and the mountains. Up above, the sky was empty of birds. Higher still, the sky was a mixture of white and blue, and the sun was an oily smudge.

The shop where the sewing class took place was in the main street, not far from the square and the fountain. About ten girls attended the class, the same ones who, later, in the evening, would set off on their bicycles to learn how to be pastry cooks and return bearing cakes and pies. When Paulo arrived, the girls were preparing dozens of decorative ribbons, as broad as a hand and in very garish colours, bright reds and blues and yellows. They were obviously making them for the day of Obaba's big fiesta, at the end of summer.

"He shouldn't be afraid. He's only doing his duty," I thought, looking at Paulo. He was standing, undecided, outside on the pavement.

"Good afternoon," he said finally, leaning on the sill of the open window. The breeze riffled the bits of ribbon lying on the workshop floor.

When the girls who were sewing or embroidering noticed Paulo, they all looked very surprised and hid their ribbons.

"Why are they doing that?" I thought. Then I learned that the ribbons were a secret. Until the day of the fiesta, no one must know which ribbon belonged to which girl. I saw the one Teresa was embroidering. It was red with little golden stars.

"No need to panic," said one of the girls rather mockingly. It was Carmen, the girl with the sour voice. "I doubt very much that Paulo has any intention of taking part in the ribbon race, so you might as well get them out again."

"You're quite right, I won't be taking part," said Paulo from the window.

"You obviously haven't taken after your father, then, Paulo," said the sewing teacher. She was a woman of about fifty, with very white skin, and she spoke very precisely. "Your father took part every year."

"He used to help prepare the fiesta, but he didn't take part in

83

it," Paulo corrected her, and a memory from his childhood came into his head. His father had just finished making a high wooden arch and was winding ribbons around a cylinder.

"Do you see this, Paulo? We wind all the ribbons round here so that the end of the ribbon with the ring on it hangs down slightly."

"I see," he had said.

"Right, well, what we have to do now is place this great big thing on top of the arch and then cover it with a plank. That's the important thing, to make sure that the only thing you can see is the ring."

The memory began to fade, but Paulo had grasped, more or less, the nature of the ribbon race which his father was explaining to him. It was a game in which the boys from Obaba, armed with a wooden lance and mounted on their bikes, would try to spear a ring and pull down one of the ribbons. Those who managed this won a double prize: the ribbon itself and the invitation to dine or to dance which each ribbon carried with it in a little pouch, along with the name of a girl.

"Are you just going to hang around at the window, Paulo? Your brother isn't quite so shy," said the girl with the sour voice, pointing to a corner of the workshop out of sight.

"It's him I've come for," said Paulo. Then he went over to the door and into the shop. I flew over and perched on a sewing machine near the window.

"I don't know if you'll get him to move from that chair. I only managed it with Teresa's help," said the sewing teacher to Paulo, and the girl she had named smiled nervously. Daniel, meanwhile, was eyeing them mistrustfully. He had a bit of red tailor's chalk between his fingers.

"Daniel, come back home with me," said Paulo, wondering how long it had been since Daniel had had a wash. Probably several days. The bunch of roses that the sewing teacher had placed in a vase could not disguise the smell of sweat emanating from his brother.

All the girls in the workshop were waiting. Daniel gave no sign of moving.

"Home, Daniel!" Paulo shouted, going over to him and grabbing him by the arm. It was useless. Only Daniel's head moved slightly. He looked like an ox trying to shoo away flies.

"We've enjoyed your company," said the sewing teacher, smiling, "but it's time you went home now. Besides, we'll be closing soon. Your friends have got to go off and make their cakes."

Paulo was getting more and more agitated. He could not bear the way the girls were looking at him. The smell of his brother's sweat penetrated to the very centre of his brain.

"I said home, Daniel!" he shouted, again grabbing his arm.

"No!" roared Daniel, hurling the piece of red chalk down on the floor.

"Daniel, do as your brother says," shouted the sewing teacher, taking him by the other arm.

"Forgive him. He's not been himself lately," Paulo whispered to the sewing teacher.

"Get off me! Filthy pigs!" screamed Daniel, wrenching his arms free from their grasp. The sewing teacher was thrown backwards and would have fallen if the girl with the sour voice had not caught her.

"You don't know how to treat the poor boy. You least of all,

Paulo," said the girl. "Daniel," she went on, "would you like to come for a walk with Teresa and me?"

"Yes . . . Teresa," said Daniel. His lips were wet with saliva.

The sewing teacher called for silence, and the girls' giggling abruptly stopped.

"I'm sorry," said Paulo to no one in particular. "We'll leave now."

Teresa got up and opened the shop door.

"Don't worry, Paulo," she said. Then they all went out into the street, Daniel laughing and everyone else grave-faced.

I left my perch on the sewing machine and flew over to the fountain. I intended to stay there, drinking the water and enjoy-ing the cool until Paulo and the others passed by. But no sooner had I alighted on one of the iron railings surrounding the fountain than I was dazzled by something very bright. The water, the spout, the mouth of the carved stone face out of which the spout protruded, the moss growing on the stone, everything that had been there before me a moment earlier was suddenly gone. I wanted to escape from the dazzle and fly away, but my wings would not respond.

"What's happening to me?" I thought, frightened. Then I remembered one of the stories I had heard other birds tell in the past:

"If ever you are dazzled by a bright light and cannot move, then resign yourself to dying. That bright light is the sign of the snake."

"So the snake is going to kill me," I thought. Shortly afterwards, I felt an intense pain in my head and then nothing.

# THE SNAKE TAKES UP
# THE STORY AGAIN

*Preparations for the fiesta*

IT WAS A CIRCULAR fountain with a square pillar in the centre, and I was lying coiled amongst the weeds that grew around the pillar with the sun full on me, and I was filled with such a feeling of intense pleasure that, if I may put it like this, in somewhat metaphorical form, not even the orders of my inner voice could have made me budge. For it wasn't just the warmth or, rather, the fire penetrating my skin and entering my blood that imbued me with strength, it was the sound of the cool water too. Now and then, a dog would come to the fountain to drink, and then, such was my confidence, I almost hoped it would find me just so that I could do battle with it.

After a while, I began to feel hungry, and my thoughts kept circling around one point, that is, whether or not it was worth bestirring myself to go in search of food and thus have to leave that delicious spot. I had not yet reached a decision, when a bird arrived and started drinking from one of the spouts. I told myself it wasn't possible, I could never be that lucky, it was one thing catching a trout, but quite another catching a winged creature that could fly away. However – this was definitely my lucky day – the bird seemed very thirsty and was so absorbed in drinking that it didn't notice a thing. Before it knew what was happening, I had hypnotised it. When it stopped struggling, I squeezed its body and split open its head. Pure joy.

I had just finished gulping down the bird, when I noticed something. A group of people were coming down the street. In front was a big lad with a big head and a girl who kept waving her arms about as she talked; behind them came Carmen with a fair-haired boy with dark circles under his eyes.

"Follow them!" I heard the voice say.

"Now? Just after eating?" I said. Nevertheless, I quickly obeyed. I followed the group as best I could and listened.

"What's wrong with you, Paulo?" Carmen was asking the boy. "You can see what's going on, can't you?" she went on, when he didn't reply.

"I don't know what you're talking about," the boy said at last.

"Daniel's crazy about Teresa, that's what's going on," cried Carmen, laughing gleefully.

"That's just gossip. It's a lie."

"A lie? You must be joking!" exclaimed Carmen vehemently. Then she pointed to the couple at the head of the group, the boy with the big head and the girl waving her arms about. They had already crossed the square and were about to turn up an alleyway.

"You just want to screw things up for Daniel," said the boy in a tone of voice I would never have expected from him.

"Who's 'you'?" said Carmen stopping at the corner of the alleyway and turning to face him.

"Teresa's mother has been talking to Don Ignacio. According to her, Daniel should be put away in an institution. And that's

90

what you all want. You want to drive him mad so that it will be easier then to get him locked up," said the boy. He was very tense.

"Look, I think you're confusing me with someone else," said Carmen, frowning. But she was pleased. "What dear Don Ignacio may think is one thing, but what I think is quite another. Don't get the two things muddled up."

The way in which the girl with the mark on her face, that is, Carmen, said "dear Don Ignacio" was just perfect. Thirty per cent mocking, thirty per cent scornful and forty per cent superior. The boy hesitated, uncertain what to say, which was hardly surprising.

They walked in silence along the alleyway, one of the few shady places in Obaba at that time of day.

"Can Daniel ride a bike?" Carmen asked suddenly.

"He's too clumsy for that," said the boy.

"I know he's clumsy, you just have to look at him," said Carmen, pointing at the boy with the big head, who at that moment was lolloping across the bridge like a toad. "But I think it would be a very good idea if he learned. You know what I'm thinking, don't you?"

"Why do you want him to take part in the ribbon race?" asked the boy abruptly. He wasn't a complete fool.

"Let me explain, Paulo," said Carmen, speaking now in a low, grave voice. She was a real actress. "Daniel is a child. Despite the fact that he's nearly twenty, he's still a child. And like any child, he needs a sense of achievement. He needs, for example, to win a prize and feel that he's the best in the world and have something to brag about for a few days. He'd soon forget about the girls then. And Don Ignacio would forget all about having him locked up."

"What do you want? For Daniel to win a ribbon on the day of the fiesta?"

"Exactly. He'd be absolutely thrilled, winning a ribbon in front of everyone in the village."

"That's impossible," said Paulo, turning and looking down into the river. They had reached the bridge to which the alley‐way led.

"No, it's not," said Carmen vehemently.

"I don't see how someone who can't even ride a bike could possibly manage to get one of the ribbons down from the arch. Daniel is too clumsy."

"Let's walk on a bit, Paulo," said Carmen, continuing along the path that led to the sawmill and then on up the hill. "It's just a matter of applying our intelligence in order to achieve our objective."

I was exhausted from so much slithering along, and I decided to stay by the bridge. It was obvious that the girl with the mark on her face, Carmen, would get her way. She was the sort of person who always did. Mentally, I begged the voice to accede to my desire for rest. The voice did just that and much more. It gave me precisely the order I had been hoping for.

"Go down into the river," it said.

I shivered with pleasure as I slipped into the water and immediately swam down to the deepest part where I hid under a stone. Once safely ensconced there, I forgot about everything else, about the comforting sun, about my desire to hunt, about Carmen's scheming, and I fell asleep.

A murmur of voices woke me up. By then, the waters were dark.

"It's Carmen and the other girl. They're coming back from the sawmill," I thought.

"Go up onto the bridge again and listen," the voice said, and I obeyed at once. After my rest, I felt light and happy.

"He's all for it," Carmen was saying in her persuasive voice. "He's agreed to teach him to ride a bicycle in time for the day of the fiesta and to train him up for the ribbon race. Everything's working out fine, Teresa. Don't look so serious."

The girl who waved her arms about gave a bored sigh. She was angry.

"What exactly is working out fine? I'm sick to death of Daniel! Whenever he talks to me, he spits all over me, and as if that wasn't enough, he's always trying to touch me up. Like I said, I've had enough!"

"Don't be stupid, Teresa, just be patient. Just wait until Daniel wins that ribbon and everything will be all right."

"Paulo hasn't even spoken to me," said the girl, letting her arms drop by her sides.

"He's just shy. Anyway, you wouldn't talk like that if you knew what he'd said about you."

"What did he say?"

"He said you're very pretty."

"I don't believe you."

"All right, he didn't say it in so many words, but that's what he meant."

"Oh, yes."

"Anyway, it isn't true he hasn't spoken to you. You talked to him a bit at the end."

"Only a bit."

The girl pulled a face and fell silent. For my part, I was beginning to feel hungry again, and my thoughts drifted off to the toads who had begun croaking near the river. The conversation between the two girls was beginning to bore me.

"I wonder what colour I should make the ring on my ribbon?" said the girl, sighing. She seemed incapable of speaking without either gesturing or pulling faces or sighing.

"I don't understand that question," I thought. I learned then that not all the girls put silver rings on their ribbons, but larger, coloured ones. That was their way of showing that they were engaged to one particular boy and that the ribbon belonged to that boy alone.

"You choose a colour and then we'll talk to Paulo."

"Do you think he'll come and have supper with me? Because, of course, if Daniel gets the ribbon with the invitation and then Paulo doesn't turn up . . ."

"What do you mean 'doesn't turn up', Teresa?" said Carmen, laughing. "Why do you think we're going to all this trouble? To spend the evening with Fatso? No way. I'll make sure you and Paulo are left alone."

"Don't worry, I'm not going to waste this chance. As soon as we've eaten, I'll tell him how I feel. And if people think it's wrong of me to take the initiative, to hell with them," said the girl, slicing though the air with her hand.

"To hell with them," I repeated.

"There's no reason why anyone should know anything

about it," said Carmen, smiling. Her serenity was in marked contrast with the other girl's agitated state. "They're not going to be sitting with you at your table. On the other hand, if you want to go off to some dark corner after supper, then try to be discreet. Everyone knows everything in villages like ours."

"We'll do our best," said the girl, smiling at Carmen. Since we were passing the fountain at that point, and since I was by then utterly bored with the two girls' conversation, I decided to leave them and climb onto the pillar again, this time to spend the night. Would the voice or the voice's master allow me to? I thought it would, and I was soon on top of the pillar.

I continued to watch the two girls. They went into the seamstress's shop and then, after a while, came out again with their bicycles.

As she passed by, the girl who waved her hands about said: "We're going to be late." She was pedalling hard.

"There's no need to hurry, Teresa. Even if we arrive after everyone else, our cakes will still be the best," replied Carmen.

The two girls disappeared down the road leading to the station. I closed my eyes and prepared to sleep.

# THE SNAKE'S STORY CONTINUES

*The ribbon race*

IN THE DAYS PRIOR to the fiesta, Carmen, the girl with the mark on her face, was somewhat agitated because she wanted to get hold of the ribbon her friend had embroidered for the boy with the big head and she feared some difficulty.

"I wouldn't worry," I thought, rather bored with having to follow Carmen everywhere. After all, her friend Teresa was one of those ingenuous types, extremely easy to manipulate.

It all went as I had predicted. On the eve of the fiesta, Carmen lied to her friend saying that Paulo had told her he wanted to see with his own eyes the ribbon she had embroidered so that Daniel, the boy with the big head, could take part in the race and do as well as possible, and, naturally, the ingenuous fool agreed. She let Carmen go off with her red ribbon embroidered with little golden stars.

"If you don't mind, once Paulo's seen it, I'll take it straight to Don Hipólito's house."

"Who's Don Hipólito?" I thought. And I learned that he was the judge of the race, the man charged with winding the ribbons round the cylinder on the arch.

The ingenuous girl agreed, and Carmen took the opportunity to exchange the large ring on the ribbon for a smaller one and then handed it over to the judge. Later, she went up to the sawmill and chatted to the boy with the dark circles under his eyes.

"I didn't think you'd still be working the night before the fiesta," she said, approaching the mechanical saw. The place was disgusting, full of sawdust.

"Here, we work until the big bell at the church rings. That's how it's always been," he said, without looking at her. He was sharpening the blade of the saw with a file, tooth by tooth.

"Not much longer then," said Carmen, sitting down on the trunk of an oak tree. This seemed a good idea and so I slithered over to join her. I ended up behind her, in the middle of a patch of moss growing on the bark.

"I've done my bit," said the boy. "Daniel can ride a bike now, not as well as we can, but he can manage."

"Then stop worrying, Paulo. Daniel will get the ribbon. It's a red ribbon with a black ring."

"A black ring?"

"No one else would think of using that colour, Paulo. That's why we chose it. If we'd chosen a blue ring, for example, someone else might go for it by mistake. Blues all look rather the same. What's wrong? Don't you like black? Has it got bad associations for you?"

Carmen was talking just like her friend Teresa now. She was a real actress.

"I don't care what colour it is," said Paulo. He continued sharpening the saw, only looking across at us now and again.

100

"Neither do I," I thought. I just wanted the whole thing to be over.

"Fine, then," said Carmen, cheering up. "The important thing is that Daniel should have his big moment and forget about all the rest. How has he been behaving lately?"

"Much better," said Paulo, almost inaudibly.

"You see, now that we've given him something to look forward to, everything's changed. Don Ignacio will have to eat his words. No one will lock Daniel up now."

"And, of course, I know how much that means to you," said Paulo, looking across at us, his brow furrowed. For a moment, I even feared for my life, because I thought he was about to come over to us with that file he had in his hands.

"I might be in danger here," I thought as I slithered down the bark of the trunk. As it is written, imprudence is not one of the snake's defects.

"It really hurts me that you should say that. Why do we have to behave the way our parents did? There's no reason for you and me to be angry with each other. We should help each other the way we used to before our families quarrelled."

"She's certainly not acting now. What he said really hit home," I thought.

"Who embroidered the ribbon?" he asked, ignoring her remark. "Was it you?"

"Everyone knows I don't make ribbons," laughed Carmen. But she had still not quite recovered. Her bitter laugh was the laugh of the weak. "Do you know what people say? That I'm afraid to make any ribbons because someone might choose my ribbon and then, when they found out it was mine, refuse to

101

go out with me. No one wants to have supper or to dance with the girl with the birthmark on her face."

Carmen laughed again. Then she started to her feet.

"There are a lot of stupid people in Obaba," the boy said.

"That's true," said Carmen, heading for the path. "But in this case, it's not just idle talk. That actually happened to me two years ago. A boy got my ribbon, but he never turned up at the place I suggested. I waited a whole hour for him."

"And what did you think?" asked the boy, pausing in his work. Suddenly he seemed very innocent.

"That I was a very unlucky girl," she shouted from the path.

"Leave the sawmill, leave quickly!" I thought. I was afraid Carmen might burst into tears and make a complete fool of herself.

I was just about to follow her when my whole body shook.

"What's that noise?" I exclaimed. I felt as if my head were about to explode.

It was the sound of bells or, rather, of one bell ringing out from the church tower. It must have been huge, because its vibrations made the air shudder.

"And now there'll be all the noise of the fiesta," I thought apprehensively. I decided to stay where I was, or, to be more specific, in the part of the river between the sawmill and the bridge in the alleyway, and there I spent the night and much of the following day. I didn't do much hunting, because the hubbub filling the village, especially the rockets and the bass drums in the brass bands, frightened away the trout and the birds, but, on the other hand, at least I could be quiet there. The water muffled the noise.

"Go to the square!" I heard the voice say after a while. I learned then that the ribbon race was about to begin and, leaving the river near the bridge – for that seemed the safest route – I slithered towards the square. It was terrible there. The men and women of the village were walking about in groups, talking their heads off and shouting, and the children seemed very excited. Worse, it was a cloudy day, which meant I could not rely on the strength and cheer that the sun always gives me. Keeping close to the walls of the houses, I managed to reach one of the trees in the square and slither up it.

The young man with the dark circles under his eyes and the workmen from the sawmill were putting the finishing touches to the preparations for the race, and the wretched children kept up a continual racket around them.

"I wonder where the boy with the big head is?" I thought.

I saw him at once. Mounted on a bike, he was riding round and round the fountain. He had a ridiculous way of pedalling and, of course, several children were chasing after him, hanging on to the saddle and generally pestering him. It was really extraordinary how many children there were at that fiesta.

At one point, the boy with the big head rode over to the part of the square where his brother was working.

"Are we going to start soon, Paulo?" he asked, putting one foot down on the ground.

"Don't be impatient, Daniel. I'll tell you when it's time," Paulo replied. "Have you seen where the black ring is? It's right there in the middle, can you see it?"

"Yes, Paulo."

"The only problem is it's rather small," said Paulo gloomily.

103

"So, Daniel, if you can't get it with your lance, you'll have to grab it with your hand."

"You're supposed to get it with the lance, Paulo," said Daniel.

"I know, Daniel, and I think you should try with the lance first. All I'm saying is that if you don't manage it, then it would be best to grab it with your hand. Grabbing it with your hand is pretty good too. People will still clap."

"They'll clap really loudly," said Daniel, laughing, before pedalling off again.

The race was due to begin shortly. The participants, each on his bike, were gathered at one end of the square, and the noise filling the Obaba air was growing by the minute. The children were screaming even more loudly; rockets were exploding in the sky; the bass drum in the brass band echoed down the streets; and with the bells ringing out, the din was positively unbearable.

"I just hope this ghastly business is over with soon!" I exclaimed in the hope that the voice might hear me and take pity on me. The noise was nearly driving me mad. Pure torment.

Suddenly, silence fell, or something very like silence. The people pressed back against the benches round the square to create a corridor for the participants in the race, and a man wearing a top hat, the race judge, placed himself next to the arch with a whistle in his hand.

"Even more noise," I thought, although at that moment everyone was quiet. Apart from the occasional baby, even the wretched children were quiet.

Luckily, the whistle was not too shrill. I gave a sigh of relief. The ribbon race had begun, the first participant was advancing on the arch with his bicycle and lance. Not much longer and

104

it would all be over. Stupid fiesta. Stupid mission. Then I would be able to go back to the river in search of my beloved trout.

The seventh participant was the first to get a ribbon. He was a skilful cyclist, perfectly capable of riding without his hands on the handlebars, and he slipped the point of his lance clean through the ring. The cylinder spun round, and he made off with a yellow ribbon; not, in my view, a particularly lovely thing. The crowd applauded and the wretched children screamed as loudly as if they had won the prize themselves.

"Where are Carmen and Teresa?" I thought. Then I saw them. They were in the front row, immediately opposite me.

"My legs are shaking," said Teresa, rubbing her hands together.

"Well, keep calm, nerves can be infectious," said Carmen, smiling.

"I'm going to wave to Paulo," said Teresa, waving her right hand. But Paulo, who was still standing by the arch, was looking at the throng of participants.

"It's Daniel's turn," said Carmen. "Let's see how he does."

He did absolutely nothing, if by nothing one understands making a complete fool of himself and provoking roars of laughter from the crowd. It is written that a bicycle must go neither too fast nor too slow, too fast and it will crash into some wall, too slow and it will fall over; but, as is only natural, the boy with the big head was ignorant of this theory. When he reached the arch, he braked so hard that he fell to the ground as if someone had yanked him off the bike with a rope. Bicycle and lance went their separate ways.

"Get that arse of yours off the ground!" shouted the man

playing the bass drum, encouraging the boy with the big head to get up. Everyone laughed, and it was rather funny.

"Paulo!" called Carmen, when the laughter had died down a little. But he didn't respond. He seemed preoccupied.

"I'm sure he'll get the ribbon when he comes round again," said Carmen.

She was, of course, lying. She thought, as I did, that the boy would be quite incapable of getting the point of the lance through the ring. And so it was. Time passed, the judge blew his whistle again and again, more and more ribbons were carried off, and meanwhile the boy with the big head failed over and over. In the end, only one ring hung from the arch, the black ring intended for him.

Most of the competitors got down from their bicycles and joined the crowd in their eagerness to follow the boy's man-oeuvres. They were truly comic, because, of course, they weren't what one would normally describe as "manoeuvres", there was nothing ordered or harmonious about them, they consisted of an endless series of falls, tumbles, grabs at the handlebars, stabs at the air with the lance and other such clowning.

"This is a great fiesta," remarked one of the men who was watching this circus from beneath my tree. He was right. Apart from the main protagonist, the only other people not enjoying themselves were Paulo and Teresa.

When this had been going on for rather too long, one of the boys in the square grabbed a competitor's bicycle and lance and rode confidently towards the arch. Before Paulo or the judge could stop him, he had stuck his lance through the black ring, and the only ribbon left on the cylinder, red with

106

little golden stars, fluttered in the air. The crowd burst into applause.

"Mine!" yelled the boy with the big head, getting off his bike and baring his teeth like a dog.

"Stop it, Daniel!" shouted Paulo.

Too late. Daniel lifted up his lance and brought it down as hard as he could on the boy who had taken the ribbon. He did so not once, but several times, and he kept hitting the boy even when the boy was lying on the ground. It took three or four men to subdue him. He was screaming like a pig and struggling to free himself from the men holding on to him. Even though they knew it wasn't true, people kept shouting that he had killed the boy. You know how it is, the sight of blood always shocks people, even when it's only a matter of a broken nose or a split lip.

"I can't understand why they let him take part in the first place. He's like an animal. He should be sent to prison," said the man leaning against my tree.

"I don't know about prison, but he certainly belongs in an insane asylum or a hospital," said a woman.

"At last," I thought joyfully, "I can go back to the river!"

# THE WILD GOOSE'S STORY

*The final journey*

THERE WERE ONE HUNDRED and eleven of us geese altogether and we had spent many days flying across the sky, heading south. We kept flying and flying, never tiring of flying, stopping only at lakes or rivers to drink and eat in the shelter of the rushes and the reeds, and even then only briefly, ready to fly off at the slightest sign of danger, be it a gunshot, the barking of a dog or two men talking.

Since I was the guide for the whole group, I was constantly alert to changes in the sky, to the brightness of the sun during the day and the positions of the moon and the stars during the night, and in that way, by the most direct route, I was leading the other geese southwards. I was not deceived by the clouds or the changes in climate or the different landscapes we saw as we passed. I followed my route unerringly, flying and flying, never tiring of flying.

When we reached the first mountains, it began to rain, and we arrived in the land of Obaba with our wings drenched. It was then that I heard the voice inside me.

"Go at once and kill the snake," it said.

I flapped my wings hard and rose up above the other geese. Realising what was happening, the goose flying immediately behind me took over and the others followed him. There were one hundred and ten geese all beating their wings in time, stretching out their necks the better to cut through the rain, flying with their minds fixed on the south. Then, very soon, they disappeared amongst the clouds, and I began to descend.

"There it is. Kill it!" said the voice, and at precisely that moment, I saw the snake. It was a black snake, hidden in a hollow on the river bed, near a bridge.

I know how to move in the air, so I flew through the air and landed on a path; I know how to move on the land, so I walked to the river's edge; I know how to move in the water, so I immediately dived down to the hollow where the snake was hiding. It lifted its head and I crushed it. Once the snake had stopped writhing, the current of the river carried it away.

When I left the water and was flying off, I heard the sound of a woman weeping. It was coming from the sawmill by the river.

"He hasn't been himself at all," said one of the men working at the sawmill. They were gathered round a weeping woman, an old woman. "I used to see him working at the saw and, to be honest, it worried me, because I could see how depressed he was, and I was even more worried when I realised he hadn't come to work today. That's why I went up to the house to see what was wrong. And when this woman told me he had gone out early taking Daniel with him, I just knew something bad was going to happen."

"That's when it all started," said another of the men. "When people started going on about getting Daniel put away."

"It's all Don Ignacio's fault. It was his idea to have him put away. And he told Paulo not to let him leave the house," said a third man.

"I don't know that you can blame Don Ignacio," said the man who had spoken first, lighting a cigarette. "After the fiesta that's all you heard in the village. Everyone was saying he should be put away."

"Where have the two brothers gone?" I thought. But I received no reply.

Since the men at the sawmill merely kept repeating the same thing over and over and were of no help to me at all, I turned slightly and flew over the village square. There I saw a man in black loudly addressing a crowd. He had no umbrella, as if the rain didn't bother him.

"We've got to form into groups and search every inch of the hills until we find them," he was saying, and the great black stain formed by the crowd's umbrellas came alive and began to move.

"No one knows where they are," I thought rather sadly.

"Look for them," said the voice.

I obeyed and I searched everywhere, flying over every wood and every hill, every ravine and every cave, I flew low and I flew high, I flew slowly and I flew three times as fast as any other bird, but I saw not a trace of the two brothers. They were not to be found there. The groups that had gone out looking for them would never find them.

Discouraged, I glided back over the village. It was deserted, apart from two girls in a street near the fountain. One of them was carrying a red umbrella, the other a white umbrella with blue spots.

113

"It's pointless. They won't find them," said the one with the spotted umbrella. "I'm sure he's gone to the station or, rather, to the railway track."

"Why didn't you say so before, Teresa?"

"Because it won't make any difference. Even if they did find them, history would only repeat itself."

"I don't know why you're being so pessimistic. You just seem to take it for granted that Paulo's going to do something dreadful."

"Of course he is," insisted the girl with the spotted umbrella. She seemed utterly sincere.

"Anyway, I'm going to tell the men who have stayed behind in the boarding house. Are you coming, Teresa?" said the one with the red umbrella. She seemed rather wicked.

"No, I'm not," said the girl with the spotted umbrella. Yes, she was sincere. And she might be right. It was possible that the two brothers were near the station.

I flew fast, at medium altitude, following the road, and I could soon make out a group of grey houses. I assumed this was the station and so redoubled my efforts. Yes, there it was. The tracks emerged from a tunnel cut out of the mountain and disappeared down the valley. The rails glinted in the rain.

The two brothers were standing between the rails, holding hands and with their backs to the mountain. Realising what was about to happen, I tried to reach them, but in vain. The train just coming out of the tunnel beat me to it.

I wasn't used to the noise of an engine like that and, for a while, I was stunned, flying around above the station, disori-ented. When I finally found the track again, I saw two geese there. One was much bigger than the other. They stretched out their necks to me asking me to guide them.

"Follow me," I said. "I know the roads of the sky well."

We left at once. Flying and flying, never tiring of flying, we would soon reach the south.

Before we left, I saw the train stopped on the tracks and several men running towards the place where the two brothers had stood.

# EPILOGUE

ELEVEN YEARS HAVE PASSED since I wrote this story and since it was published in Basque with the title *Bi anai*. In terms of my own personal history, I see the book now as a kind of second starting point in a literary career that had begun some time before, in 1972 to be precise: on the one hand, it condensed everything I had been trying out up until then – the use of imaginary places like Obaba, for example – and on the other, it forced me to invent some of the narrative methods which, like the Inner Voice, have become regular features in my fictional writing.

The book, however, made little impact. It was quite widely read in the Basque Country, and there was even an attempt to get it published in Castilian – thanks to the book's first translator, Joseba Urteaga – but it all came to nothing. Other books I wrote – *Two Letters* and *Obabakoak* – overshadowed the progress of *Bi anai* in the Basque Country, while outside it, on the other side of the wall, the silence remained absolute.

The die, it seemed, was cast, especially when, years later, I too became reluctant to draw attention to it. I had published

*Obabakoak*, and the doors seemed to be open to publishing other books too, but I feared being pigeon-holed as a writer on rural life and the fantastic. And so the years passed and the project stayed firmly on the back burner.

Finally, the moment to recover the story arrived. It took only a few words of advice and an invitation to publish it for me to sit down and rewrite it, confronting yet again the reality of the bilingual writer, a class of writer who – naively at first, and with a touch of bitterness later – tends to end up writing the same thing twice. But it's impossible to recapture that naiveté, especially when there has been an intervening period of eleven years, and the language you are writing in the second time bears little resemblance to the language used the first time: it's impossible to go back to what we were, impossible to write as we did then, impossible to find the exact word without betraying the original. And so, despite the apparent similarities, this *Two Brothers* is not *Bi anai*. In vaguely arithmetical terms, I would say that *Two Brothers* equals *Bi anai* plus-minus eleven years of the author's life.

BERNARDO ATXAGA